Free Will

A novel path to redemption

Books by Mark E. Scott

A Day in the Life series
Book 1: Drunk Log
Book 2: First Date
Book 3: Free Will

Coming Soon!
King of Peru

For more information visit: www.SpeakingVolumes.us

Free Will

A novel path to redemption

Mark E. Scott

SPEAKING VOLUMES, LLC
NAPLES, FLORIDA
2024

Free Will

Copyright © 2024 by Mark E. Scott

All rights reserved. No part of this book may be reproduced or transmitted in any form or by any means without written permission.

ISBN 979-8-89022-179-7

For Elizabeth

Acknowledgments

As always, first and foremost I want to thank my agent, Nancy Rosenfeld, for believing in me, never pulling punches, and always letting me know what's what. Invaluable, indeed.

I want to acknowledge the efforts of my editor, Elizabeth Mariner. She is a tireless confidante and collaborator, as any number of midnight texts would testify. No doubt my books are better for her relentless desire to make them so. Thank you, Elizabeth, for pushing me to get things done.

My continued, undying gratitude to the Central Cincinnati Fiction Writers, for the limitless help, friendship and advice you've all provided. Go, go, River Van Beek!

I'm unbelievably lucky to have the support of my family, and always have been. Iris, Tim, Rick, Missy, Hannah, Jake, and Lydia. Thank you all for putting up with this.

Finally, I want to thank Kurt and Erica Mueller at Speaking Volumes, from whom I keep learning and whose support made this possible.

Chapter One

Unexpected Guests

The sun was blinding, reflecting off the sparkling, virgin snow. They'd had a touch of it before, when they were inside, just through the windows. Outside, its brilliance was staggering. In its wake, the passing storm left behind a day so perfectly clear and calm, it was hard to imagine the turmoil of the previous night, but for the snow. And the cold.

An age seemed to have passed since they'd arrived at the hospital. More than an age since they'd gone off the bridge, into the river. And now here they were, about to receive a ride home from the same cop who'd, until very recently, seemed obsessively keen on arresting them for their "crimes." Those crimes had apparently been forgotten, public drunkenness and jumping off a bridge taking a back seat to hunger and exhaustion.

Life turns on its heel.

Deputy Tommie Lane quick-stepped ahead to open the back door of the cruiser for them. Jack and Aria shuffled behind him, carrying plastic bags filled with their wet clothes, still wearing the non-slip socks and scrubs they'd been handed after arriving in the ambulance, soaked through with dirty river water. The socks, however, had been rendered useless, the fibers now pregnant with the melted snow puddling under the heated entrance canopy. Within a few strides, the socks began to slide down their ankles, threatening escape, a faint slap generated by every step as the inundated material lost form and elasticity.

Jack and Aria quickened their pace, heel-toe, heel-toe, attempting to reach the deputy's car before the socks were lost completely. Had either thought about it, before they left the emergency room, they'd have dug their boots out of their bags and slipped them on. Damp boots had to be superior to soaking socks.

Nearly barefoot, they arrived at Lane's car and slid into the back seat. Without comment, each started rooting around the bags. Dripping socks were replaced with relatively dry boots and left on the floor of the cruiser almost before the vehicle started moving.

Lane pulled slowly away from the curb and weaved his way through a cohort of hospital workers at the end of their shift. Feeling like criminals, Jack and Aria stared at the hospital employees through the windows of the cruiser, wondering if they thought the same, or cared at all. As the car crawled through the parking lot, they recognized a few of the people with whom they'd crossed paths in the last eight hours. The emergency room doctor, the sleepy pharmacist, and the crew of the ambulance were all taking their leave. When Aria spotted Nurse Rita, she attempted to roll down her window to say goodbye. The attempt failed. The window controls were disabled in the back seat of the cop car. It was just as well; she wasn't one hundred percent sure Nurse Rita would welcome any further contact with her former patients. She'd already done enough to help them, having even bought them breakfast.

And delayed their blood alcohol test.

And declined to have them committed.

What more could they ask of her?

"Jack. It's Nurse Rita." Aria pointed at the nurse as if she were pointing at the Grand Canyon, visible only from the starboard side of the plane. Aria's face almost pressed against the window. It began to fog.

"Yup. My hero." Jack felt a pang of guilt, and almost asked the deputy to stop so they could assist their savior as she swept the snow from her windows. But he didn't ask, believing, like Aria, she'd likely had enough of them. They could do her no greater favor than to leave her alone.

"I mean, damn, the snow looks so beautiful."

Jack and Aria heard the remark, startled by its source. The deputy's head was on a swivel, taking in the clean, white blanket covering the earth around him.

"What?" Aria blurted unintentionally; her voice tinged with surprise.

"Hey, I *notice* things." Lane defended his humanity. "I *appreciate* things."

"Oh . . . sure. Of course. We were just doing the same."

Jack gave Aria a thumbs-up, admiring her quick reaction time, keeping his thumb below Lane's line of sight.

After a minute of waiting the deputy pulled slowly into traffic, leaving Jack wondering why he hadn't taken advantage of his siren and lights, but wasn't about to inquire. He assumed it was likely against the rules to do that sort of thing, even when traffic wasn't cooperating with official business. Lane had proven himself a stickler for the rules.

The accumulated snow was slowing the surge of drivers, all anxious to depart the hospital lots and return home to bed. Jack and Aria, relieved of the responsibility of getting from point A to point B, had time to stare out the windows and be struck by how normal the world appeared, though neither vocalized the observation. Jack took a moment to scribble it down in his notebook, which had been stuffed in a pocket of his scrubs.

8:05 (according to the dashboard clock)
The world looks normal. Why does it look so normal? I feel like everything should be different.

I mean, the world IS different now, isn't it?
We're getting a ride home from the guy who wanted to arrest us.
It's snowing before Thanksgiving.
I'm still alive, despite my best (worst?) intentions.
And now Aria and I are riding together in a cop car.
Things are definitely different, different than they were yesterday.

Given how odd the last 16 hours had been for Jack and Aria, how bizarre, each expected the world to, perhaps, take notice. They somehow expected, or even desired, the world to provide them with some tangible acknowledgment of the challenges they had faced, and overcome, together. But no such acknowledgment was, or would be, forthcoming. The world was too big, too concerned with big things, things bigger than them. Jack recalled the last scene of *Casablanca*. It was true: the problems of two little people didn't amount to a hill of beans in this crazy world. Jack and Aria had thus far survived their adventures and maybe survival was enough. And love? Jack looked at Aria's profile as she stared out the window. Perhaps . . .

"Hey, are you guys hungry?"

Deputy Lane's voice interrupted their contemplations and returned their attention to the back seat of the cruiser. Jack was suspicious. Lane's behavior over the last eight hours was not that of a man who wanted to make friends and influence people.

"Oh, no, but thank you for asking. Nurse Rita bought us breakfast in the hospital before we came down to find you."

Jack's comment was greeted with silence while Lane formulated a response.

"Wait. Are you telling me that mean nurse bought you both breakfast?"

"Um . . . yeah. I know it sounds crazy, but she turned out to be pretty nice."

"Well, I'll be damned. I don't know. She was pretty mean to me all night." Lane paused before speaking again, almost under his breath. "Seems to me if she was so nice, maybe you could have helped her clear the snow off her car."

Jack's guilt returned, now mixing with Aria's and filling the back seat with the agitation they felt at not having done the right thing and, secondarily, having that pointed out to them by a man they still weren't sure they trusted.

"Well, I really did think about it." It was Aria's turn to sound defensive. "I just figured she'd had enough of us."

Lane laughed out loud. "For sure. For sure. Okay then, let's drop it. I'll bet she's already on her way home, speaking of which . . ."

Jack and Aria leaned forward, almost involuntarily, waiting for Deputy Lane to finish the thought. It was slow in coming.

"Where am I dropping you?"

For a split-second Aria suspected he was trying to trick them. They'd given him and his partner that information hours earlier. Didn't he have it written down somewhere? Aria gave Jack a puzzled frown and he returned the look with a slight shake of his head and squeeze of her hand, indicating it was best not to antagonize the man giving them a ride home. They shared their addresses with the lawman.

"I'll get you there."

Jack and Aria, though trepidatious about their evolving relationship with the deputy, couldn't help but feel comforted by his confidence and clear sense of direction. Lane navigated the car and the urban terrain covered in an elegant blanket of white, slid by, broken only by foot and paw prints delineating the hidden sidewalks. The world was quiet, the snow absorbing sound and keeping people inside. It was not at all unpleasant.

Jack and Aria stared out the windows at opposite sides of the same street, transfixed by the landscape. Moving from one stoplight to the next, fighting sleep, the beautiful sameness wrought by the snow induced a sensation like they were gliding through a glossy, black-and-white photograph of a city they barely remembered from the day before. Leaning back, heads resting and bodies relaxed, they took in as much as they could, believing *this* morning to be the most beautiful they'd ever experienced.

"Fuck."

Lane cursed as the car shimmied on the steep, slippery hill. The startled couple abandoned the view and huddled in the middle of the back seat as the cruiser faded from the center line toward the cars lining the curb, but Lane managed to regain control, his ability impressive given the icy road and the steepness of their descent into the city.

"Everything's okay, guys. No worries."

Deputy Lane spoke but kept his attention on the road.

"Smooth sailing from here."

Jack and Aria probably should have been more concerned, considering there was still a good bit of hill for Deputy Lane to negotiate before the street leveled off. Jack and Aria lived in Cincinnati's "basin,"—a flat area near the river comprised of downtown and historic districts ringed by steep hillsides. Having posted himself in the hospital all night, it was reasonable to assume Lane was as exhausted as they. But Jack and Aria, neither able to muster more than an inkling of real apprehension, again relaxed. After all, they were not behind the wheel. They were not in control and did not wish to be, believing they would be delivered safely to their front doors because logically it did no good to believe otherwise. Not that logic had played a commanding role in the last sixteen hours.

Their trust in the invisible hand of fate, it turned out, was not misplaced. From the moment of the near-miss and onward, Lane pulled it together, guiding his vehicle with the utmost care, arriving unscathed at the bottom of the hill. No one acknowledged this success, at least not in words, but as they waited for a turn signal to turn green, sighs of relief were audible.

"Aria, I'll drop you off first."

The realization was sudden, and jarring. They were close to their homes, too close, it would seem. A moment of panic and shared thought ensued.

Is this it? This anti-climax? Is this how it ends? After everything?

Jack answered her unspoken questions.

"I'll see you later today, Aria. Promise." He squeezed her hand and lowered his voice. "Let's get some rest. We need it. Is that okay?"

Aria's mind slowed.

"Yes, of course. Absolutely." She paused. "This can't be it, though. Right?"

Jack saw the uncertainty in her eyes. "No. No way."

Lane heard the intimate exchange and felt a pang of jealousy. After everything they'd been through, after every challenge he'd had a hand in inflicting upon them, they were not broken, at least not from each other. He would drop them home, as promised, and then go home himself. In the comfort of his kitchen Lane would drink his coffee and replay the events of the last eight hours, but he had no one with whom to share them.

Well, maybe Thompson.

Sergeant Thompson had, indeed, been there at the beginning. He was the one who found Jack and Aria huddling at the edge of the river.

Thompson had arrived before Lane and the other emergency workers and was the first to determine the pair were simply humans, not alligators that crawled out of a river. Thompson was as disappointed as any of them to discover that truth, hoping for something truly fantastic to sneak its way into an otherwise boring shift, full of traffic accidents and other snow-related "emergencies." Thompson, Lane understood, might be the only person he knew who would find the story of "the rest of the night," at all interesting. He made a mental note to call him later in the day, after he had a chance to get some sleep. And maybe catch a little college football.

After maneuvering through one-way streets, the cruiser pointed north on Main. Jack, meanwhile, was wracking his brain, looking for anything Aria might have divulged about herself during one of their brief conversations at the bar. He wasn't sure she'd ever mentioned the proximity of her living quarters to her place of work and, by extension his own home, but if she had he wasn't about to mention he didn't remember. Since the accident that killed his nephew a year ago, most of his mental space had been taken up with grief and remorse. He was beginning to regret this total self-preoccupation.

Lane pulled over to the curb about three blocks south of Liberty's Bar and Bottle and pointed to a four-story, teal building. The snow on the sidewalk had not been cleared and there were no signs of life.

"Is this you?"

Aria hesitated. Jack said he would call her later, that they would meet after they rested. But she didn't want to move, didn't want to leave the back seat, fearing she was breaking a cord, disrupting a stream of energy whose flow was created some 16 hours ago, when she served Jack that first Manhattan, that first drink. That's when he started writing in the notebook, the one now floating down the Ohio River. It all flooded in and she sat frozen in the back seat of the cop car. What would happen if she broke that line; what if she disrupted the pleasant dream in which she now found herself? She didn't know; she didn't want to know.

Jack guessed at her thoughts.

"It's okay. I'm right up the street. I'll come get you for lunch."

"Promise?"

Like Aria, Jack wasn't sure why they needed to go their separate ways, other than habit and/or exhaustion, but suspected sleep might be difficult if they were together. There was too much going on between them, too much to talk about and relive. And there was sex.

Aria was on the verge of acquiescing when another thought struck her.

"Jack," she hesitated, not sure if she wanted to divulge the thought with Deputy Lane so close, but she really didn't have a choice, and leaned in to whisper in Jack's ear. "Perhaps you shouldn't be alone just yet. You know, the bridge and all . . .?"

"Oh. No. No. Don't worry. This is . . . you know? This is too good to . . ."

The words escaped his mouth and Aria understood.

"See you later." She gave him a quick hug and grabbed her bag from the floor of the cruiser, pausing for a nanosecond of guilt when her eyes fell upon the sopping pile of socks. She let them lie.

Souvenir for the deputy.

Lane stood by the rear door, opened it as soon as it appeared Aria was ready to exit, and immediately jumped back into the driver's seat. He felt no desire for idle chit-chat on the cold street corner, not when his bed beckoned.

The trip to Jack's apartment, in the same building as Liberty's Bar and Bottle, took less than a minute. Seconds later, Jack, with a quick "thank you" and "goodbye" to Deputy Lane, found himself standing, still in scrubs, plastic bag in hand, on the corner in front of the bar. He walked the few steps to his door and habitually reached toward his pocket for his keys before remembering he didn't have them. When he left the day before, when he did not expect to return, he relegated his cell phone and keys to the kitchen counter, to be easily found after the fact.

The unlocked door opened with a click and a push. Jack half expected to find a panhandler, or two, sleeping on the couch or the floor and was thankful the expectation was misplaced. Still, he double-checked his bedroom before allowing himself to relax. All clear. Finally, he stripped off the scrubs and stepped into a warm shower, the familiar surroundings reminding him why he loved his apartment. It almost hugged him, and he realized he'd not experienced this feeling in a year. Today the world *was* different from yesterday.

Aria lingered on the corner and watched Lane drop Jack in front of the bar, wondering again why she didn't stay with him, in the car, or why he didn't get out with her. She sighed and blamed the missed opportunity on exhaustion, alcohol, and the prescription medication they'd stolen from the hospital pharmacy.

Who knew it would be so easy to steal drugs from a hospital pharmacy?

Aria watched Jack disappear around the edge of his building before turning to go into hers. It had yet to occur to her that she'd left her keys in the other jacket, the one she'd traded away to Tracy the night before. That epiphany was delayed by the appearance of her building mate, Brandy, who exited the locked, exterior door just as Aria was about to enter.

"Hey! Good morning! I didn't know you were studying medicine!"

Studying medicine? What the hell is she talking about? I was just serving her and her friends in the bar yesterday.

Aria then remembered, as Brandy held the door open, that she was still wearing scrubs. But Aria didn't have the energy or desire to correct her. So she lied.

"Yeah . . . cardiology. Night shift."

"That's so cool! It's nice to have a doctor in the building."

"Not really a doctor." Aria paused. "Well, not yet, anyway."

"Still. It's cool."

Aria didn't know Brandy well, but didn't see the harm in letting her think she was a doctor, or lawyer, or ice cream vendor, as long as she cleared a path for Aria to get to her shower and bed.

"Yeah, cool. See ya, Brandy. Sorry, exhausted from all the lifesaving."

Aria ascended two floors, anxious to ensconce herself in her apartment, take a shower, and bury herself in warm blankets. She was standing in front of her door by the time she realized she had no way to get in.

Crap, crap, crap!

Think, think, think.

Aria's brain scrambled. There had to be another way in. Was it possible to get into her place from the fire escape? Yes, of course, it was possible. It was more than possible. It was easy—or should have been. She just needed to find a way to get onto the fire escape itself, and find the window she'd forgotten to lock. There was always one.

First things first. She had to get onto the fire escape. Brandy lived on the same floor as Aria, which made going through Brandy's apartment the easiest way back into *her* apartment. Hoping against hope that her airheaded building mate hadn't locked her door, Aria tried the handle, telling herself Brandy wouldn't mind her apartment being used as a shortcut to the fire escape.

The door was locked.

Plan B: Aria climbed the stairs to the other floors, stopping at every door to knock.

No one answered.

Is it possible that no one's home on a Saturday morning? Oh. Well, duh!

Aria remembered that most of the people in her building were in her age group and it was likely that most, or all, had partied until the wee hours, and were now "sleeping it off."

Think.

Aria listed her options, examining the viability of each. The first was to go back outside, to the street, and try to jump high enough to grab the fire escape's retractable ladder, thereby climbing back up to her floor.

It's too high.

The ladder floated about twelve feet above the sidewalk. Despite her history as a dancer, there was no way she could jump that high—not on her best day.

Maybe a spare key?

But she was ninety two percent sure she'd never given a key to any of her neighbors, at least not while she was sober. If one was floating around, it had been provided by one of the apartment's former occupants. In any case, she'd already failed to receive any response to her initial round of door-knocking.

Break down the door?

Her third option was born more of desperation than desire. Aria remembered seeing a sledgehammer in the basement, but immediately rejected the idea. She was in no mood to bash through her locked door, telling herself that, while the action itself might actually be fun, the consequences would be more trouble than they were worth.

So, considering her inability to communicate with the outside world, combined with her exhaustion, Aria was left with only one viable option.

Jack lived two blocks away.

She could make it, she told herself. She wouldn't freeze to death walking two blocks, despite the lack of a dry coat. Plus, she now had decent footwear.

Her boots, however, were still damp from the river, and she had no socks, so by the time she found herself standing in front of Jack's door, her toes were freezing. She rang the bell, and could hear the muffled "bing" leak out from behind the door. No answer. She rang again, worried Jack had already fallen into a sleep no doorbell had the power to penetrate. Aria, nearly resigned to a cold, painful walk back to her place and to sleeping on the hallway floor until Brandy got home, tried the bell a third time.

The door cracked open just enough to reveal a sliver of Jack, a towel wrapped around his waist. He opened the door to let her in.

John Current sat at the kitchen island drinking coffee and reading the Wall Street Journal. Susan, his wife, was still asleep—a routine they'd developed and maintained for nearly the entirety of their 35-year marriage. John appreciated the alone time. It gave his mind a chance to wander, a chance to work things out, things he couldn't work out when he was otherwise distracted. This morning he was thinking about his son, Jack, with whom he hadn't spoken in months.

John had been trying to read the same story, about GDP growth in Pacific Rim nations, for the last twenty minutes, but hadn't managed to get past the first paragraph. It wasn't that he was bored by stories about GDP growth in Pacific Rim nations. Indeed, normally he would have found the topic fascinating. But not today. Today he couldn't stop thinking about Jack, about his son, thoughts of whom were always popping in and out of his head. But today was different. Today the thoughts persisted. He needed to work it out.

Chapter Two

To Sleep; Perchance to Dream

Jack was as surprised to see Aria standing in his doorway as she was to find herself there. He stepped to the side and she passed him like a bull passing a matador. The cold had affected her more than she thought, and the blast of warm air emanating from his foyer was too inviting to concern herself with niceties. Three steps inside the door, beyond the reach of the cold, she turned and started speaking before Jack finished turning the deadbolt.

"I couldn't get into my place. My keys are in Tracy's coat . . . I mean my coat. I mean the coat I gave Tracy last night," she stammered through chattering teeth.

Aria was nervous, despite the last sixteen hours, despite what she'd learned about Jack and what he'd learned about her. Despite the sex in the supply closet. All of it seemed to have happened months ago, years ago. Now here she was in a place she'd never been, though it was only a few yards and two walls from where she tended bar.

Aria shivered, her discomfort obvious.

"It's okay. I'm glad you're here."

The shivering began to subside.

"Are you sure?"

"Of course. I should have invited you anyway. I can't believe I was stupid enough to let you get out of Lane's car."

Jack stepped to Aria and wrapped his arms around her, the warmth of his bare chest penetrating the thin scrubs.

"Listen, do you want to take a shower? Or I can get the fireplace going. Let's get you warm."

Aria considered the options through the haze of the hug in which she was enveloped. The heat passing from his body to hers was welcome and familiar, given how much time they'd spent keeping each other warm in the last nine hours. She whispered to Jack's bare chest.

"The fire sounds perfect, Jack, but a shower sounds even better."

Jack released Aria from the embrace, took her hand, and led her down the steps to the subterranean master suite, guiding her to the large bathroom where a white towel hung on a hook next to a blue terry cloth robe. Jack had stolen the robe from a Fort Lauderdale Beach hotel during spring break his junior year of college. It was two sizes too big for Aria, but it was clean, like the towel and all the clothing in the household. Jack didn't think it appropriate that his family should be forced to launder his clothes after he killed himself, so everything was washed, neatly folded, and put away.

Jack opened the shower spigot for Aria and closed the bathroom door behind him, unsure what he was supposed to do next. Until just a few minutes ago, he'd been completely focused on sleep—on climbing into his bed and forgetting about everything for the next eight or ten hours. Aria's entrance altered those plans.

Or does it?

He considered this while donning a pair of baggy sweatpants and an overlarge T-shirt. He figured Aria wanted—needed—sleep as much as he. Acting on this theory, he pulled another pair of sweats and a T-shirt out of his bureau and laid them on the bed.

Now what?

What, exactly, was he supposed to be doing while he waited for Aria to finish bathing? Was it okay for him to lie down? Should he make coffee? A fire? Get her a glass of water? Offer to wash her back?

None of those options seemed exactly right. He sat paralyzed at the end of the bed, assuming she would take advantage of the warm water for as long as possible.

The most recent iteration of the Drunk Log lay on the bed next to him, beckoning. Before he went to sleep, before Aria arrived, Jack had intended to write in it. He felt the need to write something about the bridge and Aria and the cops and the hospital, but the summary rolling around his head lacked a sufficiently coherent or satisfying theme. He'd hoped a narrative with those qualities would reveal itself to him during *his* shower, but nothing gelled. And Aria's unexpected arrival forced him to abandon the reflective and to deal with the immediate. This was fine, he told himself, opening the notebook. Though he hadn't come up with anything terribly reflective or insightful, he could still write *something*.

8:36
Well, Posterity. You should know that Aria's here now.
She's in my apartment, in my bathroom, to be exact.
Well, actually, she's in my shower.
If this is part of some universal plan, I'd love to know what the plan is.
I mean, don't get me wrong. I'm not unhappy about it. Not at all. Seriously.
True – I didn't expect to see her for a few more hours, after we both got some sleep. But this is good, even though I still want to do the sleep thing. Really. Not sure I can stress that enough.
The sleep thing, I mean.
I can hear her in the bathroom. Well, I can hear the water running.

Trying not to think about her being naked and all.
But Posterity, I mean . . . damn! What am I supposed to do here?
What's the right thing? Does she sleep in the spare bedroom? Do I? Does she sleep with me?
And I really do mean sleep. Really.
At least I think I do. We're exhausted.

Aria basked in the warm water falling on her hair, her face, and her body. The shower stall, an old coal chute repurposed, surrounded her on three sides with rock and mortar, the fourth side open, without door or curtain, so she could see the whole bathroom, and the whole bathroom could see her. Aria found this intriguing, not least so because her image was being reflected back at her by the mirrored doors of a closet, or something, located directly opposite the shower across an eight-foot expanse of tiled floor. In them she could see everything; in them she could examine her entire body, and she was pleasantly surprised by what she was able to see. Mostly. There was some damage. Especially noticeable, when she turned to look at her backside, was the slashing bruise inflicted by the river after falling off the bridge. The bruise descended diagonally from her left shoulder to the top of her right buttock. At the moment the bruise wasn't causing her any pain but some rather nasty cuts—gleaned from encounters with floating debris in the river—were making her pay for using soap and water on them. She tried not to think about it. The shower felt too good, even with a little sting here and there.

Hair and body washed, Aria lingered in the stream of clean, warm water, allowing herself to relax. She closed her eyes and listened to the splash of the water on the rock walls; she breathed in the mineral aroma of the limestone. It reminded her of a French Chardonnay they served at the bar. She had the big bathroom to herself and though the door was shut, part of her hoped Jack would walk through it, unannounced, to find her on full display. She knew there was little chance of that happening. As far as she could tell, that sort of move wasn't his style. Hers, maybe. She imagined their positions reversed—knew she would walk right through the door. No knocking required.

Aria decided she'd spent enough time basking and that Jack was not coming in. She turned off the water and gingerly toweled dry, performing a final examination in the mirrored doors before wrapping herself in the pilfered hotel robe. She was proud of her dancer's body, strong and athletic—the cuts and bruises would heal. Her hair, however, needed some attention and, after a quick search, she located an adequate brush in a drawer under the sink. A minute later, satisfied she could do no better under the circumstances, Aria exited the bathroom to find Jack sitting on the edge of the bed, staring at the door.

Jack heard Aria turn off the shower and put the notebook on the nightstand at the side of the bed, the side on which he'd grown accustomed to sleeping. The right side. Jack didn't know the particulars of Aria's sleeping habits, and there'd been no sleepover guests since before the accident, but he'd never grown accustomed to occupying all the available space of the queen-sized mattress, so half had gone unused. Plus, he liked to read in bed, and there was only one nightstand lamp. It was on the right side.

Aria's entrance cut short Jack's contemplations on potential sleeping arrangements. She was wearing the robe he'd given her and was lovely, her hair wet and brushed back, hanging down her back over the robe.

"Are these okay to sleep in?" Jack waved his hand over the sweatpants and T-shirt he'd laid out for her.

"Sleep?"

Jack flushed. "Well, I didn't want to presume . . ."

Aria laughed.

"I'm sorry, Jack. I'm joking. Right now, all I want to do is sleep." She was lying for Jack's sake. The shower had washed away some of the exhaustion. "Thank you for these."

Jack's shoulders relaxed as Aria slid into the improvised pajamas.

"Can I sleep here?" Aria was pointing to the right side of the bed. "Or do you want me upstairs in that bedroom?"

Confronted with the possibility of actually sleeping in the same bed as Aria, Jack blanked on an answer. He reminded himself they'd already defiled a storage room at the hospital, but somehow that seemed different. As opposed to sex in a closet, lying in bed and sleeping next to Aria seemed vastly more serious, vastly more intimate.

Aria laughed. "Jeez, Jack. Lemme make this easier for you. What side am I sleeping on?"

"Uh, yeah, of course. You take the left side, okay?"

"I'm going to assume you mean here." Aria was pointing to the side on which she thought Jack was telling her to sleep, the side holding the notebook and the light on the nightstand. His side.

"Um, sure. You know, 'stage left' and all that."

Jack had no idea how to determine stage left or stage right or, for that matter, port or starboard. He'd neither spent much time on boats nor ever been involved in a stage production of any kind. He was just doing his best to keep the words flowing and maybe not look like a total jackass. He wanted to know if his brutal awkwardness registered with Aria, but could not examine her face. He'd turned his back to her while she changed out of the robe, but turned back in time to see the bruise before she pulled the shirt all the way down. He'd first seen it in the emergency room and now it looked even more painful, the color deepening from red to purple.

Without hesitation, Aria finished dressing, pulled down the bed covers and slid between the sheets, her fluid movements apparently unaffected by the river's damage.

"Let's get some sleep."

Without thinking, and without feeling the need to think, Jack followed orders and climbed in next to her. He laid on his back, staring at the ceiling, arms at his sides as if he were standing at attention, or lying at attention. It was all so abrupt. The whole moment. Whatever was happening between them was still happening, but the magic and spontaneity of the storage closet had by now dissipated, replaced by fatigue and nerves. To Jack, the whole scene seemed an odd combination of relationship newness sprinkled with the nonchalance of a couple who'd been climbing into bed together for years. He froze, suddenly fearful that whatever he did would be wrong and, by doing so, would ruin everything. So, barely breathing, he closed his eyes.

The fucking light is still on.

Aria, on the other hand, fought to hold back a giggle, wondering if she'd just crawled into bed with a serial killer. She'd never seen Jack so awkward and stiff, and wondered at the effect she was having on him. After all, she was the one who'd just showered in a bathroom she'd never seen before, a weird shower, too. A bit like showering in a cave. A cave with mirrors. Standing in the artificial downpour, she couldn't stop looking at herself in the mirrors. Weird. And now she was in Jack's bed, in his clothes. She was the one who should have felt awkward.

But, she admitted to herself, the sweats *were* warm and comfortable, and so large as to make her appear shapeless. Feeling safely ensconced, she now wanted nothing more than to be right where she was.

Indeed, she couldn't think of anything more satisfying than the thought of lying beneath Jack's covers in his big clothes. She wanted to sleep and figured if Jack were, in fact, a serial killer, she'd likely be dead already, her body stuffed into a secret chamber under the basement floor.

She burrowed further into the covers.

She was on her side, facing Jack. His eyes were closed, his body rigid, like he'd strapped himself to an invisible slab of plywood hidden beneath the sheets. Aria allowed her hand to escape the blankets and placed it on his shoulder. He said nothing, but she could feel his body relax.

"This mattress is really comfortable, like it's hugging me. Is it one of those purple ones?"

"Uh-huh. Purple."

Aria pulled herself closer to Jack, molding her body to his, close enough to note the shower had removed the rank river odor in which they'd steeped for hours, and replaced it with a clean, soapy scent. Her body fell into his as her mind began to drift, eyes closing as she gave in to sleep.

"Is this okay?"

She asked as if from the edge of a dream, her voice separate from herself.

"Perfect." He sounded far away.

Jack felt Aria's body press into his. He was happy she was comfortable but couldn't remember the mattress color. For all he knew, it was Paisley. But now was not the time for a discussion on mattress technology. He would correct the lie later. Maybe over lunch.

Aria had drifted off. He heard her breath go shallow and felt her body slump into his. He was torn. He didn't want to move her but wanted to turn off the light. It was on the nightstand, and there was no way to reach it without disturbing her.

It's fine. I can do it. I can sleep with the light on.

And he could. Jack sank into the mattress, felt the weight of the blankets push him down. He found the combined pressure of the blankets and Aria's body comforting and, even with the light on, he could no longer fend off the sleep that had been chasing him on and off for hours.

Aria, asleep first, dreamt of her sister Steffi, as she often did. Steffi's suicide haunted her and in the dream they were children. Aria, as an older sister would, was teaching Steffi how to swing higher on the playset in the backyard where they'd spent a good part of their childhood.

Steffi laughed as Aria barked instructions and pushed her from behind.

"Now kick your legs forward."

Steffi had never swung so high, and every swing took her higher—so high the chains started to go slack at the top of the parabolic arc she'd created. At the tippy top of the arc, Steffi turned to look down. She wanted to see how far above the ground she'd gotten, but as she turned, she lost her grip. As gravity brought her and the swing hurtling back to earth, Steffi fell forward, landing face-down with a thud on the dusty ground beneath the swing.

Horrified by what she'd witnessed, Aria believed her sister dead or terribly injured. She'd just watched Steffi come down hard from the heavens, and now her sister lay motionless, arms and legs akimbo. Aria knew she should check to see if her sister was still breathing but was afraid to do so. What if she was actually dead? What would she do then?

It was her fault, Aria knew. She was the older sister. She was the one teaching Steffi to swing. A helpless wail arose in her chest, but as the scream threatened to escape, Steffi laughed.

"Do it again! Do it again!" She'd already jumped up and was climbing into the swing, using the chain for leverage.

It took a moment for Aria's voice to return, a moment for her gut to stop feeling punched. "Jesus, Steffi, I thought you were dead."

"Don't swear, Aria. Mommy doesn't like it. Now push me again!"

Aria did as requested and started pushing, though not quite as hard.

She woke from the dream with a start, heart beating fast.

Just a dream. Just a dream. Breathe.

She was shaken, but grateful it wasn't one of the really bad ones—one of the ones where Steffi kills herself. She didn't know how long she'd been asleep but knew it couldn't have been long. As her heart slowed, she realized how wonderfully warm she felt in Jack's clothes, under his covers. His bed was more comfortable than her own, and she made a mental note to ask him about it again, at a time it made sense to do so. She was still pressed against him. He was breathing loudly, almost a snore but not quite, and the lamp was still lit on the nightstand next to her. Gently, so as not to disturb him, she rolled over to turn it off, and saw the notebook.

On a whim and now fully awake, Aria left the light on, grabbed the pad and sat up, propping her back against the pillows and the headboard.

8:52 AM (according to that clock you've got on the wall above your bed)
I just had a dream about Steffi. You and I haven't had much time to talk about my sister but I dream about her a lot. This one was not the worst. We were kids. She was tough. But

they aren't all like that. The dreams. Before I write any more, I just want to remind you that we're both exhausted and that I can't be held responsible for what I'm writing here. It may make sense, but it may not. I'm just doing some rambling.

The thing was, a lot of the time it was just the two of us, me and Steffi, I mean. Mom and Dad always told me that since I was the older one, I was supposed to look out for her when they weren't around, like somehow an eight-year-old is going to understand what it means to take responsibility for a six-year-old.

I say that now, but I think I actually did get it, and as I got older it made more and more sense. And Steffi would let me, you know, watch over her, if that's even the right way to say it. She never really fought me about it, but it's not like I was super-mean or super-strict. Neither were Mom or Dad, I guess. Maybe we should have been. Maybe it would have been different.

Probably not.

Enough for now.

Aria slid the pen into the wire binding, set the notebook on the nightstand, and settled herself into the bed, pulling the covers over her shoulders. In her weariness, she'd forgotten about the light. But she didn't want to move and rationalized the light wouldn't keep her up, and Jack, as far as she could tell, was sound asleep. She lay staring at the white ceiling, tracing the color change as the lamp light faded from white to yellow, until it was swallowed by the shadows creeping in from the corners of the room. Finally, she closed her eyes, hoping not to dream.

Jack had drifted off but the feel of Aria wiggling under the blankets was enough to wake him. She was no longer spooning him, but he still felt the heat of her. Eyes still closed, he listened. He could hear her breathing, but just barely, and not enough to overcome the sound of the silence. The quiet was palpable, thick—a slight buzzing in his ears. The buzzing wasn't unpleasant, just enough to keep him from going back to sleep and, besides, thinking about going to sleep only served to wake him further. He began thinking of things he could be doing other than lying awake in bed.

Wake up Aria?

He rejected this immediately, believing that any touching, even a gentle tug on her shoulder, would likely be construed as an opening salvo for sex. Jack didn't think that a bad thing, not necessarily, just that the timing was wrong. They would have sex again, he believed, but he wasn't sure when or under what circumstances, or who would initiate the sex, or where they would be, etc. Before Jack knew it his id had taken over his ego and all he could think about was sex. But, having decided not to paw at Aria, he found the sex thoughts annoying and tried to put them out of his head. None of his usual brain tricks worked. He tried silently singing *Julia* by the Beatles but couldn't remember the second verse. Then the song garbled in his brain and transformed into *Why Don't We Do It In The Road*, the words of which were easier to remember, but still problematic. Now he had to find a way to banish not just the sex thoughts, but the Beatles earworm as well.

What to do? What to do?

Jack opened his eyes and gently brought himself to a seated position, thinking a little walk around the apartment would be enough to help him regain control of his brain. Before he had a chance to swing his legs over the side of the bed, he saw the notebook. It was still there, on the table, close to Aria's face.

Free Will

Doing his best not to disturb her, Jack deftly reached across Aria and grabbed the notebook, quietly turned the sheets of paper to the first blank page, and saw Aria's entry.

How the hell did I miss that? Was I actually asleep?

Intrigued, he wondered if it was okay to read what she'd written, and rationalized that, yes, it was. It was his notebook, after all. If she wrote in it, she would know that he would read it. And this had already happened in the hospital. In all likelihood, she expected him to read it.

He was right. It had been written to him, only minutes before.

John made one more attempt to focus on the news story, failed, and refilled his coffee cup. The guilt had been gnawing at him for months. Yes, Troy's death was tragic. Yes, Jack was responsible. Yet he loved his son. Nothing could change that. John had been struggling with this for nearly a year. The whole family struggled with this. And now he couldn't concentrate enough to read the paper. He could only stare out the window, sip the coffee, and hope the universe would show him a way out, that the universe would relieve him of this burden, let him off the hook. The worst part was that John already knew the answer, what the answer had to be. He just didn't know how to get there . . .

Chapter Three

Coffee, Tea, or Me

Jack wanted to respond to Aria's log entry, and this desire effectively banished the Beatles, for which he was grateful. It wasn't the Beatles' fault—he had to think about what he was going to write, and the thinking was burning through his (currently) meager supply of brain power. He understood she'd shared something personal with him, an important insight she may have never shared with anyone else. But even if he hadn't been the first to hear about this, it didn't matter. What was important was that she *wanted* him to know, and that whatever he wrote back to her in the log had to honor that.

Jack flipped through his brain's filing cabinet of memories, opening drawers and closing them, looking for the perfect thing to say, the perfect response. He found what he was looking for in a file hiding somewhere between his hippocampus and cortex.

9:02 (I'm using the wall clock also.)
I read what you wrote to me a few minutes ago.
We're in and out of sleep, and I'm wondering if you're awake right now.
I don't think you are.
I can see your eyes fluttering, like you're dreaming.
But don't worry, I'm not just sitting here staring at you,
not that that would be unpleasant.
Creepy staring aside, I wanted to share something with you, too.

Free Will

When Troy was three I took him to the zoo.
I remember he was constantly in and out of the stroller, one of those folding kind you use for toddlers.
I tried strapping him in but every time I did he just got pissed and started screaming,
so eventually I gave up.
I didn't want to be that guy whose kid is screaming, everyone judging.
It was much easier to let him get in and out of it on his own, or just let him do whatever he wanted and chase after him when he escaped.
I mean, he wasn't crawling into the ape cages or anything like that.
I always stayed close enough to grab him if it looked like he was going to do something stupid.
One of the things he really liked was when I spun him around.
What I mean is that I spun the stroller with him sitting in it.
The first time I went slow. I think we were somewhere around the zoo train station, and he had just climbed back into the stroller. Like I said, I started slow at first, but he liked it so much I started dialing up the strength of the spins.
We'd walk around and he'd go, "Spin me! Spin me!"
So, I spun him. I spun him maybe five or ten times, over and over again.
Until he flew right out of the stroller.
You see, I forgot he wasn't wearing the seat belt.
He refused to wear the seat belt, and I let him get away with it.
He flew out of that stroller like he'd ejected from a jet fighter.
I watched him fly five or six feet.

I watched him land, face down, on the dirty pavement. Scariest moment of my life.
I thought I killed him.
And then I heard him laughing.
He hadn't even rolled over yet. He was still face down when he started laughing.
"More! More!" It was crazy. He thought it was fun.
I told him no way, of course, and thanked God he didn't have a scratch on him.
I didn't bother to tell his parents, and the crazy part was that he didn't either.
He was only three but he made it our secret.
I don't know. I think my brother would have thought the whole thing was funny.
His wife, not so much.
But now I'm convinced that kids are made of rubber.
It's the only way to describe their survivability.
Maybe I don't believe that anymore.
I still dream about him, you know. Just about every night.
Whether I want to or not.

Jack stuck the pen back into the binder and laid the notebook down, hoping what he'd written would resonate with Aria, hoping she would feel the connection. He looked down at her. She hadn't moved while he was writing, and now part of him willed her to wake up. Only part, however. He really did want to talk to her but wasn't sure how conversational she'd be after just, he guessed, 23 minutes of sleep. He decided to leave her alone, gently slithered under the covers and closed his eyes, falling asleep quickly.

Now they were both dreaming, bodies paralyzed by brains trying to repair themselves after the night's labors. They were touching, but just barely, shoulder to shoulder, neither aware.

Now they were in and out, each waking for subtle seconds before dropping back into sleep, and never at the same time. They couldn't stay asleep, and they couldn't stay awake. Too much had happened to them, between them, in the last 17 hours and the stimulation of it all had thus far failed to dissipate to a level that allowed them to remain in the depths. The staccato journeys in and out of Neverland were blessedly absent of Troy and Steffie apparitions, populated instead by more or less benign moments from the bridge, the snowstorm, cops and paramedics, and other memories lifted from their internal highlight reels. However harmless those memories kept drawing Jack and Aria back to the surface, demanding to be recognized and categorized by minds trapped in an exhaustive, mental ballet of catch and release. Deep sleep was elusive.

Aria regained consciousness. The memory of struggling to the surface of the cold river brought her back from the depths. Eyes open but disoriented, she searched for and found the clock hanging on the far wall of the bedroom, reckoning she'd been asleep for twenty or thirty minutes. She tried closing her eyes, not moving, hoping for sleep to return. It didn't.

She sat up, reexamining her strange surroundings. The first thing that struck was the quiet. The bedroom was in the basement of the building, the walls consisting of a 160-year-old foundation of mortar and limestone, mostly exposed but broken up with panels of painted drywall. The effect of the design choice was simultaneously frightening and calming. Frightening because she realized there were five stories of building resting on the foundation, the entire structure relying on the architectural and masonry skills of long-dead German immigrants. But

Aria was not claustrophobic and soon found comfort in being surrounded by the old rock, which allowed no outside noise to penetrate. Under any other circumstances, she would still be dreaming.

Jack lay on his back next to her, eyes closed, face aimed at the white ceiling.

What to do? What to do? It's so quiet.

Aria continued gazing around the room looking for items of interest, or really anything to take her mind off the fact that she was more awake by the moment. Upon entering Jack's place she'd noticed a rather well-stocked bookshelf in the great room upstairs, but there was nothing to read in Jack's bedroom, at least nothing visible. She leaned over to see if he'd stashed a book on the bottom shelf of the nightstand, but the only thing there was a paperback copy of *Slaughterhouse Five*.

Not a fan.

Aria couldn't go back to sleep. She was restless and wanted company in her restlessness. She decided there was only one logical course of action, even if it was a little mean.

She needed to wake Jack.

She wasn't sure how that would go. People reacted differently to being woken up. She thought it possible he might try to punch her in the face but dismissed the idea. Jack just didn't seem like a face-puncher.

More likely a hugger.

Still, she trod lightly and, placing her hand on his shoulder, doled out little shoves whilst giving her face as much distance as possible should a startled flail come hurtling in from Jack's side of the bed. But Jack was not waking easily and Aria did not want to tempt fate by shaking him harder, so she decided on another course of action, and grabbed the notebook from the nightstand. Hoping the act would settle her restlessness, Aria intended to write, but instead found herself engrossed in

Jack's story about Troy. When she finished, the need to wake Jack was even more urgent, so she placed the notebook on her lap and replicated the shoulder-shaking behavior she'd attempted minutes before. This time it worked and Jack, thankfully showing no desire to punch anything, crawled out of his slumber.

"Hey. What's up?" The tenor of his voice was down about an octave from normal. She liked it.

Aria paused. She intended to talk to him about Troy, was excited by the prospect, but balked once she had Jack's attention. She felt embarrassed and remained silent while Jack stared, waiting for her to answer his simple question.

"Are you okay?" Jack sat up to wait for his answer.

"Yeah, I mean, yeah. I'm okay. I just read what you said about Troy. I think it's the first story you've ever, well, *told* me about him."

"What did you think?" Jack wasn't sure exactly what he meant by the question. Was he asking her what she thought about the story? About the writing itself? About whether he was a good uncle? He wasn't sure and, luckily, Aria responded before he was forced to clarify.

"I liked it. It sounds like he was a cool kid." Aria squirmed ever so slightly as she referred to Troy in the past tense, unsure as to how Jack would hear it.

"He really was."

Jack, after thirty or forty minutes of sleep, felt surprisingly fortified, but wasn't sure how ready he was to dish about Troy's life and/or their relationship, at least any more than he had already. After all, nine hours earlier he was ready to throw himself off a bridge because of the part he played in his nephew's death. Polite conversation about their field trips might have to wait a while longer.

Aria recognized Jack's hesitation, and her own, and decided to change the subject.

"How do you feel about getting some coffee?"

The drastic topic change took Jack by surprise, but he recovered quickly. "Absolutely. What are you thinking?"

"I'm thinking we put on some clothes and walk over to Coffee Emporium."

"I think that's a great idea, but . . ." Jack hesitated.

"But what?"

"Well, you kind of look like a hobo. I mean, your clothes are clean and all, just oversized, like you got them on sale at Goodwill."

Aria laughed. "Well, good point. But if you dress to match then my hobo-ness won't be so obvious. I think it's only fair."

"Don't worry. I've got your back." Jack wasn't sure how "fair" it was for him to wear baggy clothes to match Aria but wasn't about to refuse. It was Saturday morning and at least half the people in the coffee shop were going to look like they just rolled out of bed. Oversized clothes would fit right in.

While Jack rummaged through his bureau, looking for baggier clothes, Aria watched silently and wondered why sex hadn't come up since she'd arrived at Jack's condo. It wasn't that she felt a pressing need, rather that the situation itself was ripe, despite their lack of sleep. She thought maybe she should bring up the topic, that maybe Jack was too embarrassed or too polite to bring it up. The sex in the hospital storage closet happened so naturally, she wondered if that moment could ever be recreated. Before she had time to overanalyze, Aria plunged in.

"Hey, Jack."

He stopped the clothing search and turned to Aria.

"Yeah?"

"Well . . . I just had a question." *Don't lose your nerve.*

"Shoot."

"Well, not to be too forward, but I was just wondering why we hadn't had sex again. I mean, here we are with this warm bed, and all we're doing is sleeping."

Jack smiled and answered carefully. "Crazy night, huh? Not sure, exactly. I think I figured we needed the sleep more than we needed the sex."

What Jack didn't say, what he couldn't say, at least not yet, was that he still wasn't sure if he was *allowed.* He wasn't sure if he was *allowed* to touch her, *allowed* to enjoy her. And it certainly wasn't that Aria wouldn't let him touch her. She would. She wanted him as well. But Jack wasn't sure he deserved it, not after Troy. He wasn't sure he'd yet finished paying the penance for his sin. What happened in the storage closet was a fluke, he told himself. They were caught up in a moment.

"I'm not really sure how things are supposed to go now."

Aria smiled, admitting to herself that she wasn't quite sure, either.

"Okay. Maybe coffee is a good place to start the day again."

Jack relaxed and turned back to rummaging.

"Sure. Let's add more caffeine to the drug mix and see what happens."

He threw a pair of dry socks at Aria and pulled on the clown pants he'd worn for Halloween three years earlier. He couldn't find the clown shirt but managed to fish out an old, oversized, distended sweatshirt he usually wore only when he wasn't feeling well.

"What do you think?"

Aria gave him a once-over and laughed.

"I think you look worse than me. I think it's perfect."

Jack led Aria up the steps into the foyer, where they donned their damp boots. The dry socks made a difference, at least until they absorbed some of the boots' moisture. It had occurred to neither that they could have saved themselves the fashion embarrassment had they bothered to wash and dry their river clothes while showering, writing, dreaming, and sleeping.

The morning sun had disappeared, now hiding behind storm clouds. It wasn't snowing but felt like it should have been. It was still early, and few of the sidewalks had been cleared, so they mostly walked in the streets, covered only with a fine layer of powder after the city's overnight efforts to clear them. The unexpected snowstorm had provided everyone in the neighborhood a good reason to spend the morning inside, and not many denizens yet braved the cold. A few adventurers were out enjoying a walk in the still-clean white of the new snow, and all looked less frumpy than Jack and Aria.

In spite of the slippery pavement, they quickly covered the three-blocks to Coffee Emporium, choosing not to dawdle in the stiff, cold breeze. The interior was warm and the space cavernous, at least for the average coffee house. Jack and Aria knocked the snow off their boots on the entrance carpet and followed the directional arrows printed on the floor. The trail led to a girl with a shaved head and pants nearly as baggy as Jack and Aria's. Their order was simple enough, consisting of two large coffees and two bananas.

"That'll be seven dollars." The bald girl was attentive, but couldn't stop staring at Jack's pants.

Aria reflexively searched her pockets for money before remembering her wallet was in the zippered pocket of the coat trapped at Tracy's house. She shot a pained expression at Jack, who searched his own pockets for cash while the bald girl wordlessly prayed that when one of Jack's hands reappeared, it would be dragging a string of handkerchiefs behind it. It had been a slow morning and any entertainment was welcome. But Jack was searching for the bills he'd stuffed into one of the oversized pockets before they walked over. He had more than enough money to pay the disappointed cashier.

They took a seat at the hightop bar that ran along the wall beneath the windows. Sipping coffee in silence, they stared through the frosty panes, each retracing their separate paths of the previous night; paths that crisscrossed this neighborhood—Jack in search of deliverance, Aria in search of Jack—until they finally came together on the bridge. They'd survived the leap into the frigid water of the Ohio River. Now, stunningly, they found themselves sitting across from each other, sipping coffee and nibbling at bananas, as if nothing extraordinary had happened to them or between them. Jack broke the silence with a simple question.

"Are you okay?"

"Do you remember what it felt like?" Aria continued to gaze out the window.

"Which part?" Jack was not trying to be flippant. There were, after all, a lot of parts making up the whole of their evening and morning. He just wanted to be sure he was answering the right question.

"Hitting the water."

"Wow. Hell, yes. Of course. It was so . . . stiff. Hurt more than I thought it would."

Aria brought her eyes back to Jack. "Thank you for jumping in after me. I can't believe you did that."

"You would have done it for me." Jack smiled, knowing she would have. "I'm glad I did."

"It was pretty heroic."

Jack smiled. "Well, let's not blow things out of proportion. I mean, I was going to jump anyway."

Aria managed to swallow a mouthful of coffee before laughing.

"True. At least I didn't ruin it for you. Not really, anyway. After all, you still got to take the leap, even if I beat you to the punch."

Jack reached across the table to wrap his fingers in hers. He was hoping to again sit in silence but was distracted by the people around them. It wasn't that they were loud or boisterous. In fact, to a person they were quiet as church mice, speaking in hushed tones so as not to interfere with the hushed tones of their neighbors. Perhaps they were telling secrets they didn't want heard and feared their words too easily bounced off the concrete floor and walls and thence around the room. In any case, the crowd was subdued, so it wasn't the lack of noise stealing Jack's attention away from Aria's hand. It was the normality. Everyone seemed so ordinary, but not in a bad way. Not necessarily. To Jack they seemed ordinary because most, or all, likely never experienced anything close to what he and Aria had the night before, and now they were all just sitting around drinking coffee, discussing the mundane, or so Jack assumed.

He sat in wonderment at the thought, but then realized he may be completely wrong. He realized he had no idea what anyone around him was talking about, and that it was quite possible any, or all, of them might have bigger tales to tell than he and Aria. But he doubted it.

"Jack." Aria's voice crept into his musings. "What are you thinking?"

"Do you think anybody here has a story like ours? I mean, from last night?"

Aria glanced around the room and pondered the question before answering.

"No way. Well, maybe that girl in the dress."

Jack smiled and took a sip of his coffee and allowed his mind to move on. In its fatigue, he was not inclined to ponder one thought for very long. And while he enjoyed wondering about the stories of the surrounding coffee drinkers, he figured he and Aria should probably take this time to deal with more concrete items, like figuring out how to get her back into her locked apartment. They had yet to formulate a reentry plan.

"Do you have any way to get hold of Tracy?"

"Why? You trying to get rid of me?"

Jack wasn't quite sure how to answer, even though the answer was, of course, "no." He didn't want her to leave, subconsciously fearing the emotional hole her absence would create. At the same time, he didn't want to seem too adamant that she stay, lest he cast himself in a somewhat less-than-sane light. It did not occur to him to ask her how she felt about it but, had he done so, he would have been pleased with her response, and learned she would not think him at all insane.

"No . . . no. Of course not. I just didn't think you'd want to be without your phone for too long."

Aria took a moment to respond. She hadn't thought about her phone for at least an hour and, even though some of that hour had been eaten up in sleep mode, she was still surprised how easily she was able to let go of the thought of it, how she hadn't felt the need to have the phone attached to her hand.

"You know, I'm kind of okay without the phone right now. Besides, the only person I'd call is Tracy, and she's the one who's got my phone. Plus, I don't even know if it still works."

"Do you know Tracy's number?"

"Oh, God no. Do you know anyone's number?"

Jack laughed. "Outside of my own, no."

Aria punched Jack lightly on his shoulder.

"Well, damn, Jack. You're a genius. I know mine, too. Hopefully, the battery is not dead and Tracy will hear it. Maybe she already found it in my coat pocket. Can I use your phone?"

Jack did not have his phone, either. It was still on the kitchen counter. Neither had used a phone since the day before.

"Sorry, didn't bring it. We can try when we get back to my place."

Aria nodded but was unable to muster much excitement about getting her phone back. Like Jack, her mind wandered and turned its attention to the line that was building at the cash register, the length of which seemed to double while she stared from across the room. The clock behind the counter read 9:27 which, on any other day, might seem late for a morning coffee rush. But she took note of all sorts of people, including, but not limited to, a hardy runner or two, more than a few young women in pajama bottoms, and a couple of police officers. Other than the cops, nearly everyone in line seemed in need of a shower, and one patron in particular distinguished herself from the pack.

"Jack." Aria pointed to the young woman in a short party dress whom she'd noticed earlier. Her up-do had sort of melted over from its original, top-of-the-head position and was listing dangerously to starboard, ready to give way at any time. Her ankle boots, while attractive, offered little protection from the half-foot of snow on the ground. "What do you think her story is?"

Jack performed a cursory examination and felt bad for her.

"Walk of shame, for sure. I feel like I want to go over there and give her my pants."

The young lady, while clad in a warm, woolen overcoat, had left her legs bare. She was not shivering, but looked as if she might begin at any moment.

"Your awesome clown pants? Do you think she would take them?"

Jack glanced down at the red polka dots. "Probably not."

Free Will

John stared down at his coffee cup, still half full despite the thirty minutes that had passed since he poured it. His mind was working to solve a problem of the heart: How could he reconcile his love for his son with the fact that his son caused the death of his grandson. He knew there was an answer and, in fact, already knew it, even if he didn't know how to get there. The path was murky, but the mist was beginning to lift. He decided to warm his coffee and give his thoughts more time to percolate.

Chapter Four

"What the hell?"

Jack leaned in and whispered the words to Aria.

"What's going on?"

"That guy over there at the counter—I think I heard him say our names."

Aria looked to the counter in time to see a pink-haired girl at the register shrug and shake her head "no," at which point she took possession of what appeared to be a business card the man was handing her, no doubt with instructions to call him should she happen to run into Jack Current and/or Aria Balfour. The whole scene sent a chill up her spine. It was her turn to lean in.

"Do you recognize that guy?"

The "guy" was dressed in a suit and overcoat and looked a little too professional for a Saturday morning at Coffee Emporium.

"No, but he looks like a cop, or maybe a reporter, doesn't he?"

Aria nodded in agreement.

"Do you think we should get out of here?"

"Maybe. Maybe we can slip out behind him or wait until he leaves."

Their coffee time having been interrupted by the mysterious stranger, and the polka-dot pants discussion having run out of steam, Jack and Aria silently bided their time, waiting for the man and his overcoat to leave the premises. But he didn't leave and instead wandered the floor, perhaps considering asking the other patrons if they knew anything about Jack and Aria. They had no idea how long he planned on staying around, so instead of waiting for the cop/reporter to exit, they slipped out the door as soon as his back was turned, trying to

Free Will

look as inconspicuous as possible in their loud togs. But as far as they could tell, no one was paying attention to their movements.

The youngish man in the poorly tailored suit waited his turn before addressing the pink-haired girl behind the counter. Her name tag said "Lydia."

"Yes, hi Lydia. I'm a reporter for The Enquirer." He paused after the introduction, waiting for some sign of recognition to cross Lydia's face. When none was forthcoming, he continued. "I'm River Van Beek, and I'm following up on a story about some people who live in the neighborhood. I was hoping you could help me."

Though the pink-haired Lydia was, in fact, looking directly at the reporter, there was no sign acknowledging his request. None. "Cool name. Um, did you want some coffee?"

River released a shallow breath of frustration. "Yes, I like your name, too. Okay, sure. I'll take a caramel macchiato."

"What size?'

He was struck by the possibility the pink-haired cashier was better at her job than he at his. She, after all, had managed to pump him for enough information for her to input an order, while he had yet to glean even a modicum of whatever knowledge she might be harboring about the local inhabitants. Having earned his grudging respect, he gave her what she wanted before resuming his line of questioning.

"Large, please."

While the cashier wrote River's order on the side of a large paper cup, he examined his surroundings. The dining area was nearly half-full, occupied by people in various conditions of dress, some more alternative than others. The most interesting were a couple in baggy clothes, the male actually wearing what appeared to be clown pants, covered with polka dots. A pub crawl, perhaps?

"That'll be $4.50."

River fumbled for his wallet but paused when he remembered why he was in the coffee shop in the first place. It wasn't for coffee.

"Hey, listen. Do you know anyone who lives around here named Jack Current or Aria Balfour? I'm following up on a story for the . . ."

The cashier was already bored with her customer and the line was beginning to build behind him. "Who?"

"Jack Current and Aria Balfour. They live around here, I think."

"No. I don't think so. I mean, they might live here and I just don't know it. I don't know everybody's name." She shrugged.

"No, of course not." River assumed she forgot the names as soon as they were written on a cup. "Do you mind asking your friends real quick?"

While River fought to get the information he desired, Jack and Aria slipped out. River didn't notice them leave. He was too busy dealing with Lydia, who was somewhat less-than-enthusiastic about the prospect of annoying her coworkers with the question. But, in the end, she got lucky. One of the baristas knew of Aria, and even walked over to River to impress him with this knowledge.

"You're a reporter?" The barista was taking no chances. For all he knew, River could be a stalker, or serial killer, or tax collector.

"Yes. For The Enquirer." River pulled a laminated identification card out of his pocket and displayed it for the barista, who gave it a cursory once-over without really examining the details. The fact River's picture was on the card was enough.

"Okay, well, I know Aria's a bartender over at Liberty's and Jack hangs out there a lot. You can try asking about her over there, but I don't think they open until two. I'm pretty sure Jack lives in the same building, behind the bar." The barista chuckled and mentally patted himself on the back for being so helpful.

River smiled. He'd stumbled upon his first really solid piece of information.

A welcome blast of cold washed over Jack and Aria. They hadn't bothered to take off their outer layers inside the coffee shop, and the heat had built up between the thick layers of their clothing. Without a word they turned the corner to make their way back to Jack's, whose apartment was starting to feel like a quasi-version of "home base," and not just because their choices of destination were limited. The option of Aria's apartment was still on the horizon, so long as they could devise a way to gain access. But all that didn't seem to be part of the consideration of home base. It was more the fact they had, through challenges overcome, become a team, and had already begun to trust one another, in every situation, no matter how bizarre.

Aria grabbed Jack's hand and placed their combined, double hand into the pocket of Jack's overcoat.

"So, what do you want to do today?"

She was being playful even as she grasped they had some important issues with which they had to deal. So, they walked and talked, discussing the merits of one action item or another. And as they shared thoughts the agenda came to include washing their clothes, getting Aria into her apartment, contacting Tracy to recover Aria's phone and getting some sleep. But, thus far unspoken, was the most important item—figuring out just what they were to do with each other from this moment forward.

The last item, of course, would prove the most difficult, requiring far more time than was allotted to them on the short walk back to Jack's, far more time than they had on that one wintry day, or the next, or the next after that. Jack and Aria instinctively knew this to be true, could sense it with every fiber of their overworked nervous systems, and so concentrated on small steps. By any rational measure, the ordeal of the last ten hours easily justified a day in front of the television, doing nothing more than drinking coffee and eating cinnamon rolls. But not now. There was work to be done.

The small steps would be undertaken. Loose ends would be tied. Small, careful steps on the slippery snow would lead to small, careful steps across the threshold of Jack's apartment, and so on, and so forth. And it was in this way, in this pattern, they journeyed the few blocks to his place. As they had on the walk over, they stuck to the street as long as cars were not careening down upon them. The uncleared sidewalk was preferable to getting pancaked by a rolling chunk of steel.

The wind had calmed during their time in the coffee shop, and now the sky began to release more snow.

"The flakes seem bigger."

Aria felt buzzy. The caffeine was kicking in and mixing with leftover alcohol and the Modafinil they'd consumed during their time at the hospital. It was not an unpleasant feeling, though she wasn't sure if the light-headedness was more the result of the mixture of drugs or another wave of exhaustion.

"Yeah, I guess they do."

Jack hadn't noticed the size of the flakes until Aria mentioned it and didn't really know if they were larger than they'd been earlier. But he agreed with Aria because he'd become inclined to trust her, to trust the things she said. Even if it was only about the size of snowflakes. In fact, he'd learned he didn't really need to question her judgment at all. So far, between the two of them, they'd run any number of gauntlets and arrived home unscathed. Well, sort of. There was definitely some scathing, but it was temporary. The physical wounds would heal.

Jack's phone was still sitting on the kitchen island when they re-entered the warmth of his apartment. "Hey, have you thought of a way to get hold of your friend if calling your phone doesn't work?"

"Actually, I think I have."

"Really? Fantastic. What are you thinking?"

"Well, while we were sitting in the coffee shop, I spent a little time trying to remember more phone numbers."

"And?"

"And the only number I could remember was my mom's. But here's the thing. I'm willing to bet she's got Tracy's phone number on *her* phone. So, all I have to do is call her from yours and hope she answers."

"Good thinking. But . . . do you really want to call your mom and explain how Tracy ended up with your phone?"

"Oh, God no. Of course not. I'll just tell her Tracy and I switched coats because mine was wet from falling, which is the truth. The rest I'll totally lie about, or try to avoid altogether."

"Well, you know me. I'm all in for a good lie. The bigger the better. But, hey. I think I'm a dumbass."

"Hmmm . . . You might be, but why do *you* think you're a dumbass?" Aria poked Jack playfully in the stomach.

"I think I might be a dumbass because it occurred to me, just now, that I have a car."

"Okay, well, so do I. What's your point?"

Jack poked Aria back. "Now who's the dumbass? Allow me to explain. Like you, I have a car. Unlike you, I have keys to a car. Therefore, ipso facto, we could actually *drive* the car to wherever Tracy lives, retrieve your phone, get your keys, and trade your coats back. Genius, right?"

Aria laughed at her own blind spots. "Damn right it's genius. Why didn't I think of it?"

"Well, there's the dumbass thing . . ." Jack playfully poked her again.

"There is a problem, though."

"What? Are you worried I don't know how to drive in snow? Are you afraid I gave my car away before I tried to kill myself and then forgot that I did that?"

Aria frowned, ever so slightly. It hurt her to hear him say it out loud. She knew it was there, that it had been there all night. His plan to commit suicide, after all, was the reason they were both out in the storm in the first place, but she said nothing. Even if she didn't like hearing the words, she thought it better that he was willing to say them. Somehow, saying the words took some of their power away, some of the fear.

"No, Jack. This sounds stupid, but I don't know where Tracy lives. Not anymore, anyway." Aria paused. "It's my fault. After the first baby was born, they moved to the 'burbs, and, you know, I was dealing with a lot and just never went to see her at the new place. I mean, I know the neighborhood, sort of, but I couldn't pick her house out of a lineup."

To Jack, Aria's transgression hardly seemed worth the guilt she was exuding. He communicated with few people from his college days and almost none from high school. He stared at Aria, wondering if that was the right way to respond, by telling her he didn't really have any friends from the "old days." He decided against it. Clearly, she was not happy with the way she'd allowed her friend to slip away. But Jack recognized an opportunity to get to know her better, something he desperately wanted to do.

"So, how long have you known Tracy?"

Aria seemed startled by the question. Surprised.

"Wow. Okay. Well, I've known her since we were six, since our first dance class together. Funny."

"What's funny?"

"It's funny that you asked about it, you know, something sort of mundane, after all . . . this." Aria swept her arm over her outfit and then made the same motion over Jack. "It seems like such a normal question."

"Well, normal seems kind of good right now."

Aria smiled. Jack was correct. Normal was exactly what they needed, even if they couldn't quite afford it. Not yet, anyway.

"So, do you think I should just, you know, call my mom?"

"Or . . . and I'm just spitballing here . . . or we could take my car and go drive around the neighborhood where you think your best friend lives, hoping we'll recognize a car, or a mailbox, or catch her in the driveway shoveling snow. You never know. We could get lucky. Plus, it would save you a potentially embarrassing call to your mom, although I'm not sure what we're wearing is any less embarrassing."

Aria, touched by Jack's offer to drive randomly around Tracy's neighborhood, performed a quick cost-benefit analysis on both plans of action: the phone call or the drive-around. She decided against the drive-around. Tracy's neighborhood was the sort where all the houses looked pretty much the same, so much so that on previous visits, undertaken years earlier, it was necessary to count the houses from the corner to make sure she pulled into the right driveway. She knew if they didn't catch Tracy or her husband outside, the chances of identifying their cookie-cutter tract house were slim.

There was something else, too, another argument against getting into Jack's car—they would have to leave home base. This was not something she wanted to do. She felt safe with Jack, cocooned in his apartment with the weird shower and comfortable bed. She liked it there and they'd already left and come back once. At this point, the last thing she wanted was a potentially aimless drive-around. It would surely break the spell.

"I think I'll bite the bullet. I'll call my mom and tell her as little as possible. I don't want to leave here again until we're sure where we're going."

Jack understood Aria's dilemma and, by extension, his own. But, as much as they might enjoy it, they couldn't just spend the day lollygagging around his house. Yes, his condo offered the basics needed for a comfortable human existence. But his dwelling was lacking the little extras that, he assumed, women liked to have around. Things like makeup and moisturizer, and their own clothes. These were things he was sure could be found in abundance in *her* apartment. Certainly, gaining access to her closet had to be a priority.

"Okay, of course. You're right. What's your mother's phone number?"

Aria recited the number to Jack, who handed the phone to her when it started ringing. The call went to voicemail after eight rings.

"Mom, it's me. I'm calling from a . . . friend's phone. I need you to answer next time I call. Or call me back at this number."

Jack remained silent as Aria set the phone down on the counter. It didn't bother him to be referred to as a "friend." How, exactly, was she supposed to refer to him without sowing confusion and questions? He was positive that in the near future he would be granted a title worthy of their importance to each other. "Hero" came to mind, but he would be happy with "boyfriend."

"We'll give her a minute or two. She doesn't answer if she doesn't recognize the number, but she'll listen if there's a voicemail."

"Same for me."

Jack and Aria stood, staring at each other in silence, the status of the phone suddenly taking on oversized importance. They looked at each other, then at the phone, then at each other, back and forth, expecting it to ring at any moment, almost willing it to do so. When it became apparent that staring at the phone would yield nothing, Aria picked it up and redialed her mother. This time Mrs. Balfour answered, and Jack bore witness to one side of a (mostly) awkward conversation.

"Yeah, it's me, Mom."

"No. No. I'm fine. It's a friend's phone."

"No. Yes. No. He's standing right here."

"The friend. The guy that owns the phone. He's standing right here."

"Yes. It's a guy."

"His place."

"Because I can't get into my place."

"Because Tracy has my keys."

"Because they were in my coat and we traded coats last night."

"Because mine was wet and Tracy felt sorry for me. She's got my phone, too."

"Mom . . . Mom . . . Mom. I don't want to go into all that right now."

"No, I don't want to go into that right now. I just need Tracy's phone number so I can call her and get my stuff back."

"Yes, you do. It's in your contact list. Just go to your contact list and read me her number."

"Yes, you have it. I'm sure you have it."

Jack grabbed a pen and a pad of Post-It notes out of the junk drawer on the kitchen island and slid them in front of Aria. She wrote down a number.

"Thanks, Mom."

"No. Yes. I'll call you later."

"I will. I promise."

"No, I'm fine. Really."

"Okay. I'm going to call Tracy now. Thanks, Mom."

"No, I have to call Tracy now."

"Love you, too."

Aria dialed Tracy, phone in one hand, sticky note in the other. Jack was in thrall. He couldn't believe he was allowed to be part of this process. He hadn't talked, literally hadn't talked, to his mother for almost a year. Not since he'd killed Troy. He'd almost forgotten what those conversations sounded like.

"Tracy, it's me."

"Yeah. Yes . . . I did."

"Yes . . . I'm standing here with him now."

"Tracy . . . Tracy . . . Tracy. Yeah, we can talk about it later, okay? I was calling because you have my phone and my jacket and my keys and, of course, I need those things."

"Really? Do you think it's working?"

Aria put her hand over the receiver and whispered to Jack. "She put my phone in a bowl of rice. She says it turns on and it might work."

Jack pumped his fists.

"Yeah, Tracy. That sounds great. I'll see you in a few hours. You're the best."

Aria handed Jack's phone back to him. "Okay, well, she said she could meet us at Liberty's at two. She's not home now but she'll swing by the bar after she runs some errands. I think she wants to meet you."

Aria gave Jack a playful punch on the shoulder while he contemplated potential conversation topics that might arise upon his first meeting with Tracy. *Oh, no, I really DID want to kill myself. What? You're asking why I DIDN'T kill myself? Well, I guess I'm not as good an engineer as I thought, or maybe I'm just unlucky. What? Well, I mean maybe the bridge isn't high enough above the water. I mean, both of us survived the jump, so . . . What? Well, I killed my nephew. Yes. Basically, I killed my nephew. That's why.*

Free Will

For her part, Aria was pleased with the results of her conversations with her mother and Tracy. She'd anticipated them as train wrecks, especially if she was forced to go into detail about her time with Jack. She wasn't quite sure how she pulled it off, the lack of detail-providing, and hoped to avoid a full recounting of her recent adventures for, well, the rest of her mother's life.

A wave of calm washed over her. At first, she didn't understand what it was. It had been so long, years, since she'd had a similar experience. Not since Steffi's death, she reckoned. The decompression that came with the wave made her sleepy, but only for a few moments. Tracy wouldn't show up for another four hours and no matter how much she wanted to get things moving, no matter how much she wanted to exert some control over the current situation, she really couldn't. Under the circumstances, she'd done as much as she could do. For now, anyway, she remained pleasantly stuck in Jack's clothes.

What to do? What to do?

She took Jack's hand, led him out of the great room and down the steps to his bedroom. Sitting him on the bed, she pushed him down and climbed onto him, straddling his waist.

"Could we do some laundry?"

John figured he'd spent more than ten minutes sitting on the toilet, long enough for his legs to start going to sleep, and the prickly feeling was enough to force him out of the bathroom and back into the kitchen, where he was again confronted with his worry and an empty coffee cup. The latter was easy to fix. The coffee in the urn was still warm, but he needed something more, something to take off the edge. John explored the liquor cabinet next to the refrigerator and pulled out the bottle of Kahlua. It was exactly what he needed, he told himself. Now he could think.

Chapter Five

"Fuck the laundry," said Aria, still straddling Jack, pulling off her top. Wrapping themselves around each other, their desire to touch, to hold, to bond, momentarily overcame any other consideration.

Their lovemaking was emotionally intense but physically tentative, enthusiasm for the act itself tempered by the pain of their recent ordeal. Each movement, each touch, was a small torment: a flexing of muscles bruised and sore, a collision of skin abraded and stinging. As anxious as they were to be together, the ache and irritation were difficult to ignore. Kisses and caresses needed to be carefully placed. Winces and grimaces co-mingled with sighs, adding to the awkwardness of their inexperience with each other's bodies. It was evident this was *not* a pleasurable kind of pain for either one—neither could say it "hurts so good."

The encounter was certainly not *all* bad, yet each wondered why they had not been aware of all their bodily damage in the storage closet in the hospital: perhaps the drugs and alcohol had masked it or some of the soreness had yet to set in. And being the first time and in unusual circumstances, dopamine and adrenaline likely played a part. But now, when they had all the time in the world—or at least four hours until they had to meet Tracy—the pain and exhaustion were getting in the way of what should have been pretty great sex.

Wordlessly and mutually deciding it was time to cease and desist, they rolled apart, still holding hands. Just which of them had achieved more success in this encounter was a matter of perspective. Jack, totally relaxed, immediately started to doze. Aria, on the other hand, was too wired, too tingly, too sexually charged to sleep. She would've liked to snuggle with Jack and make small, intimate talk in avoidance of all the heavy things in their hearts, but she knew they needed sleep. There would be time for talking later.

She could tell Jack was out. His breathing changed and his hand jerked in hers, the muscles reacting to randomly firing synapses in his head, his body still lapsing into a deeper sleep. She envied him. She was tired but knew she wasn't going to fall asleep, no matter how long she lay supine, or tried to relax her mind and body, yoga-like. Once convinced her movements wouldn't wake Jack, she eased her legs out from under the covers and over the side of the bed.

The room was warm enough, at least if one was wearing clothes, which she was not, and covered in a fine sweat, she felt a chill as she emerged from the covers. Her temporary togs, removed by Jack some minutes earlier, were still in a pile at the foot of the bed. She shook off a shiver, separated "her" clothes from Jack's, and redressed as quickly as she could. On impulse, Aria grabbed the notebook from the nightstand, and made her way out of the room and up the steps, leaving Jack alone.

Other than the few minutes on the phone with her mother and Tracy, Aria hadn't spent any time in the great room of the condominium, and she was of a mind to explore it further while Jack was sleeping. It wasn't that she was looking for anything in particular. She just wanted to snoop and see if anything lying around would give her more insight into who he was, though she didn't characterize her search as snooping. For Aria, it was more like being on a treasure hunt without a map. She wanted—no, craved—to know more about this damaged, yet compelling young man in whose life she had suddenly become entwined. She would, quietly, have a look-see.

The first thing that caught her eye was the coffee maker. She thought it interesting that Jack had one, mostly because she didn't. She'd never bothered to invest in one. She did, after all, live across the street from a coffee shop, and rationalized it would be ridiculous to make her own when someone else was making it better right across the street. In fact, it had been so long since Aria had brewed her own coffee that she dared herself to see if she could make a decent cup of it. Right at that moment.

But Jack's coffee stash was not sitting out on any of the bamboo counters, nor was it visible on any of the open shelves. Suddenly, Aria's desire to relearn the ancient art of drip coffee-making transmuted into an excuse to open all of Jack's cabinet doors. It was, quite naturally, a perfectly reasonable search for coffee grounds but, sadly, she found them almost immediately. The 35-ounce container of Folgers sat in the center of a slide-out shelf, nestled comfortably amongst a bag of rice, canned black beans, sugar, flour, olive oil, and Doritos Cool Ranch corn chips. Aria popped one in her mouth before grabbing the coffee and coffee filters and went about fulfilling her personal challenge.

The first thing she did was clean the glass carafe. The crusty sediment at the bottom hinted at how many times the carafe had been used since its last cleaning. Aria, wishing she'd found a putty knife during her snooping, alternately scrubbed and flushed vigorously under the running water. It was the only thing in Jack's place that needed cleaning thus far, and she was happy to discover the flaw.

Once a reasonable level of cleanliness had been restored, Aria filled the machine with water, dropped in a clean filter and, guessing at the amount of coffee she should spoon into it, hit the start button. Unbeknownst to her, she guessed correctly.

Aria now had time to kill, at least as much time as it would take for the coffee to brew, and there were plenty of cabinets and bookshelves left to explore. Since she was already in the kitchen, she started with the cabinets, the ones she'd been denied a chance to open by her quick discovery of the Folgers container and was unsurprised to find them fairly well-organized. Despite the state of the coffee maker, she'd not expected otherwise. Everything was in order, especially compared to her place.

The fleeting fear that Jack might be a sloppy boyfriend made her laugh. She was certainly not the queen of organization or cleanliness. A cursory examination of her place would be enough to convince anyone of that fact, so she made a mental note not to let Jack visit her apartment until she had time to tidy things up.

Aria continued prospecting while the coffee dripped in the background.

Occupying the living room area of the great room were two chairs and a couch, all upholstered in a dark brown fabric. The chairs and couch faced each other across a leather-covered storage trunk that doubled as a coffee table. Near one end of the couch was a gas fireplace, a flat screen television mounted above it. Behind the chairs, a white, built-in bookcase spanned the entire wall, rising from the floor to the twelve-foot ceiling. It was the room's most striking feature. A rolling ladder made it possible to reach the top shelves. Aria found the whole setup a bit quaint and romantic, as if she was in a Victorian library or mansion. To the best of her knowledge, she'd never known anyone with a rolling ladder attached to a bookcase. Besides the ladder, she marveled at the sheer number of books occupying the shelves. There were hundreds of titles.

There's no way he's read all these books.

She was right, of course. Jack hadn't read *all* the books. But he'd read more than a few of them. Some of the books were his, but many more were left over from the previous owner of the condominium, who found the presence of the books comforting, even those he'd never read. For his part, Jack had no desire to get rid of them, and simply added his collection to what was already there, along with some family photos, mementos, and other doodads he'd picked up in his travels.

Aria sat on the couch, admiring the organized chaos: a vertical rhythm of volumes of varying heights, widths, and colors, occasionally broken by Jack's personal items. It was all very calming. She recognized some of the titles and authors. Shakespeare, Ian Fleming, and Hemingway were all represented, and she decided she wanted to spend more time examining what the bookcase had to offer.

When did I stop reading?

Quick flashes of memory reminded that her pleasure-reading days ended in college, where reading for this class or that class took priority over reading something she actually *wanted* to read. Aria cursed herself for letting it happen.

The shelves held more than books. They held clues. Knick-knacks, tchotchkes, and pictures filled the spaces unoccupied by the books themselves. Aria searched the curios, wondering what she was seeing. Some of the memories were obvious, though she still had to guess at their provenance: shells ferried home from a summer vacation at the beach; a geode purchased at a tourist trap somewhere in the Appalachians; a baseball signed by Pete Rose. She picked up a ceramic ashtray that looked to be made by a child and turned it over, thinking it might be a gift from Troy, and saw it was inscribed "To Dad, from Jack." Aria found the collection fascinating, offering small insights into Jack's history.

As she moved from one shelf to the next, she spotted a 3X5 wood photo frame turned to face the wall. Aria reached up to grab it, to see what she was missing, and in her hand discovered a snapshot of Jack and a little boy. The background put them at a park or maybe the zoo. They were smiling at each other, laughing, joyous even. She wished she could have been in the picture with them. She couldn't remember the last time she felt as happy as Jack and Troy looked in that photograph. She was sure she *had* been that happy, at some point; she just couldn't remember when.

Aria put the picture back on the shelf, facing the wall as before, trying to leave it exactly the way she'd found it, like she'd disturbed a shrine. She also wanted to avoid detection of her snooping.

On her right was the gas fireplace, and Aria decided her soon-to-be-poured, homemade cup of coffee would be even more pleasantly consumed in front of a fire. It took her a minute to find the on/off button, which had hidden itself behind a potted houseplant. Aria flipped the switch and, when nothing happened, she flipped it again. And again. Still nothing. Refusing to allow frustration to get the better of her, she put on her repairman's hat, confident she could fix the problem. She knew a little something about natural gas appliances. She had a finicky gas fireplace in her apartment as well.

After opening the glass doors that protected the flame from small children, animals, and drunkards, Aria identified the area where the pilot light should be.

I got this.

She dropped down to her knees and examined the guts of the fireplace. If the pilot light was lit, she was unable to spot it, so she started moving the well-used ceramic logs around, looking for the tiny flame. But the logs were covered in soot, and before long her hands were blackened by it, as was the tile hearth in front of the fireplace, where she'd allowed the gas logs to rest during her quest for fire.

Aria ignored the soot and carried on intently, finally discovering the lifeless pilot: a slender, metal tube, extending from the bottom of the fireplace up through to where the logs had been resting. But she still couldn't determine the problem. Figuring she needed to improve her angle of observation, Aria inserted her face, ever so slightly, into the firebox itself, just enough so that she was able to look down and spy a dial and, following the simple instructions thereon, managed to light the pilot before she was overcome by a not-so-irrational fear of a natural gas explosion.

Aria was proud of herself. The pilot light shone, bright but lonely, in the darkness of the black-walled firebox. Despite her general self-assuredness in things natural gas-related, this was only the third pilot light she'd ignited during her short lifetime, and so she took a moment to admire her work before carefully restacking the ceramic logs in a manner she felt would optimize the beauty of the flame.

She stood triumphant, again flipped the wall switch, and waited to be rewarded with a warm, gas-powered fire. The flames, however, were not immediately forthcoming. After flipping the switch a couple more times, Aria decided to give it another look, but did not bother to turn the switch to the off position before again sticking her face in the fireplace. It was at that moment the flames appeared. It was at that moment she nearly lost her eyebrows.

Luckily, the fire manifested itself before her whole head was completely inside the firebox, saving her face and hair from damage, unlike her eyebrows. They were singed, but not completely gone, the fact of which she was as yet unaware.

Aria felt she'd dodged yet another bullet, and was gratified by the appearance of the flame, which was so clearly a result of the log placement. Overcome by the beauty of her creation, Aria's first impulse was to run downstairs, wake up Jack, and describe her victory in vivid detail. She decided instead to allow him to remain asleep. She could regale him later.

Still standing in front of the fireplace, she looked down at her soot-covered hands. She would have to wash them before she touched anything else, so she returned to the sink to scrub away the ash, enjoying the smell of the brewing coffee which, judging by the popping sounds emanating from the machine, was nearly done.

The floor can wait a sec.

Aria grabbed a mug from one of the cabinets she'd perused on her second pass of Kitchen Exploration. On it was emblazoned, in block letters, "The Dog Likes Me Better." She poured coffee into the mug, pondering its declaration. Jack did not appear to have a dog, and if he did it was the quietest dog in the world, and very well hidden. Aria liked dogs, and was suddenly disappointed that Jack didn't have one, or didn't have one as far as she could tell.

Maybe it's in a kennel or something.

Aria returned to the fireplace, carrying her coffee and a roll of paper towels to clean the sooty floor. It occurred to her, given that Jack had intended to take his life the night before, he wouldn't have left his dog all alone, waiting to be found. That would have been cruel, which Jack was not. She made a mental note to ask him about the dog, if indeed a dog existed.

Aria sipped her coffee with her right hand and tried to clean the floor with the paper towel in her left hand, however her initial efforts to remove the soot were unsuccessful. The covalent bonds holding the thin slices of ash together quickly surrendered to the slightest touch and only served to smear the affected area. Aria was forced to retreat to the kitchen and hunt for an auxiliary weapon—a bottle of spray cleaner—which she found beneath the kitchen sink. Along with the spray cleaner, she grabbed the notebook, which she'd left next to the coffee maker. She was in a mood to write, though she had no idea what, exactly, she was going to write about.

Something will pop into my head.

Aria sipped her coffee and went about properly attacking the black smear on the hearth, the spray cleaner clinching the battle. The floor now ash-free, she rewashed her hands, refilled her mug and plopped down on the couch. She could already feel the heat from the fireplace. In the face of the radiated warmth, the comfort of the couch, and the relaxing presence of the books, her eyes began to close involuntarily, and she nearly spilled the coffee as she jerked awake.

For safety reasons, Aria set the mug on the coffee table in front of the couch and picked up the notebook.

10:25 AM
I'm tired, Jack. But not as tired as I should be, I think. After everything, those fifteen or thirty minutes of sleep I got earlier aren't enough. Surprise, surprise.
Just so you know, I'm sitting in your living room drinking coffee. I got the fireplace going, by the way. I wonder when the last time was you used it. Or if you use it at all. It took me some work to get it going again. It's on now. It's heating my feet.
I'm glad you're sleeping, even if I'm not. Have you been having trouble sleeping? I don't mean this morning. I mean for the past year. Ever since the accident with Troy. I imagine you have, but we haven't talked about that.
There's so much we haven't talked about.
I may be rambling now. My brain seems to be flying everywhere. Maybe the coffee will help me focus. It's really good. I guess I make good coffee. Maybe it's your machine. Maybe it's me AND your machine. Doesn't matter. The coffee is good.
Do you have a dog? I suppose I'll ask you that when you wake up. You know, when we're awake together, at the same time.

Free Will

Listen, if we both fall asleep at the same time, make sure to set your alarm. Tracy is going to meet us at 2 at the bar. Don't forget. She's got all my stuff. If I had my phone I'd set my alarm, but I guess if I actually had my phone, I'd already have my stuff and I wouldn't need to set my alarm. Ha! Don't forget to set your alarm, okay?

Listen, I'm really sorry about Troy. I'm sorry about the whole thing. It's a small thing to say, but I hope things get better for you. Maybe I can be part of that. The helping-things-get-better part. If you'll let me.

When we have a chance, a real chance, I'll tell you all about my sister Steffi and you can tell me all about Troy.

Don't forget to set your alarm.

Aria set the notebook down on the trunk and grabbed her coffee, which had begun to cool. She was quite comfortable and had no desire to move, figuring it would be okay for her to fall asleep on the couch in front of the fireplace.

Jack won't mind.

She drank from the mug, set it down next to the notebook, and reclined into the fabric cushions, pleasantly surprised by the aroma, or rather the lack thereof. From prior experience with the couches of single, young men, she was prepared for something rank to hit her olfactory sense. The couch could very well have smelled like man-sweat and beer-farts. But it didn't. Indeed, the couch sported a sort of new-car scent, which Aria found more than satisfactory. She closed her eyes.

Aria fell asleep quickly. She fell so fast she was dreaming within moments. In the dream she and Jack were paddling on a lake. She was at the helm of the canoe and Jack in the stern. The little boy, Troy, sat between them. He was sitting on the plastic seat but was leaning out over the edge of the canoe, dragging his hand in the water and looking for fish beneath the surface. He was wearing an oversized, orange life jacket, which he hated.

Then something happened. The kind of thing that only happens in a dream. A six-foot wave rolled toward them from the center of the lake. They saw it coming, tried to maneuver, but it broadsided the canoe before they had a chance to turn into it. The force of the wave knocked all three of them into the water. She and Jack resurfaced, Troy did not. The life jacket floated, empty and useless, next to the capsized canoe. Without speaking they dove under the water to look for the boy. Their attempts unsuccessful, they began to panic . . .

Mercifully, the condo's doorbell pulled Aria out of the nightmare, leaving her disoriented but happy to awake back to reality. The bell rang again before she had time to pull herself together, and she nearly stumbled on her way to the door.

She did not answer right away, instead using the peephole for safety. Eyeball to the hole, Aria startled. She couldn't believe what she was seeing on the other side of the tiny tunnel. It was the man in the ill-fitting suit from Coffee Emporium.

It was River Van Beek.

John believed the Kahlua was the best idea he'd had so far that day. In a fit of self-deprecation, he told himself he was very good at fixing problems that weren't really problems and allowed himself a wry smile. But he had yet to muster the courage to fix the real problem at hand, to take the first step—to call his son. But what then? He knew how to dial a phone, but what was he to do once Jack picked up? What were the right words after shunning your son for a year, for cutting someone out of your life who didn't deserve it? He stared at his phone to give the words more thought. He wanted to say the right thing. He wanted to beg for forgiveness.

Chapter Six

The River Flows

Compared to many of his colleagues, River was relatively new to the news business.

He'd majored in Journalism in college, and though he'd only managed a C average, he'd paid enough attention in class to understand the rudimentary elements of an investigation. He also understood that a good place to find a local news story was to start with the police and/or sheriff's office, both of which were kind enough to send out a daily summary of their activities over the last twenty-four hours. It was in this way that River discovered two people had emerged from the Ohio River the night before and been taken to the hospital.

The sheriff's summary of the event, while lacking personal details, included the fact that the 911 caller believed alligators/crocodiles, or perhaps lungfish, had shimmied out of the river soon after midnight. The supposition appeared to be no more than a flight of fancy on the part of the caller, but River wanted to believe the alligator/crocodile/lungfish story because, if true, it would be the most interesting thing he'd ever written about.

Regardless, the supposed species of the river-dwellers turned out to be *homo sapiens*, a fact River found somewhat less interesting than the opportunity to hunt down a stray, four-legged reptile. But he told himself that, no matter what type of creature had been detained on the riverbank, there was definitely a story there, and he was determined to get it. River was desperate to be taken seriously at the newspaper, as he had, thus far, only been assigned fluff pieces about charity dinners, ribbon-cutting ceremonies, and mayoral proclamations, each more boring than the one before.

River found these assignments less than desirable. Though he'd never found the time to read *All The President's Men* in college he *had* found the time to watch the movie version and decided, sometime during the first half, that he wanted to be Woodward or Bernstein. Or both. And he was determined to achieve this goal despite his "C" average, which he believed to be the underlying justification for all the fluff assignments. He figured, was he to be taken seriously, he just needed one good story: this could be his Watergate.

It was with this determination that he ended up in Coffee Emporium that morning, and why he ended up knocking on this particular door. The daily summary from the Sheriff only had names, but no addresses, and River was forced to snoop around the coffee shop because Google failed to help him find the addresses of Jack and Aria or, in other words, the alligators in question. However, the search engine did cough up information about Jack's accident from exactly one year before and about the death of his nephew. The tragedy further piqued River's interest, so he gathered as much information as was available on the internet and ventured out into the snow to find the connection.

And River knew there had to be one—a connection. How could there not be? The man and his nephew are in a horrific accident, and the man's nephew is killed as a result. Exactly a year later that same man jumps off a bridge. And he's got a female accomplice? To River, the whole thing smacked of suicide cult, or at least suicide pact.

But what was her story? The man's story was easy enough to put together, what with the death of the little boy. But what was *her* motivation to jump? What was *her* reason to be in a suicide cult and/or pact? His brain swam with possibilities, so much so that he felt a little light-headed from the excitement of it all, yet also more determined.

The more he thought about it the more fervent his door banging became. This story was going to be his road to better assignments and the respect he knew he deserved.

Aria stood behind the vibrating door, trying not to make a sound, though it would be hard to hear anything over the racket being made by the man on the other end of the peephole. She hoped, at first, that she could outlast him, that his fist would start aching or his arm would get tired and he would give up. But after what seemed an hour of banging, but in actuality was less than a minute, she realized her waiting stratagem probably wasn't going to work, that he seemed more determined to get the door answered than she was to *not* answer it, and decided she would have to involve Jack.

The pounding continued while Aria slipped down the steps to the subterranean bedroom and knelt by the still-sleeping Jack. Initially surprised at how much the banging was muffled by the short distance from the top of the steps to the bedroom, she stuck to the idea she needed to wake Jack. The banging was not stopping.

"Jack?" Aria nudged his shoulder and said his name clearly, but not too loudly, lest the crazed man at the door somehow hear her over the din. "Jack?"

He stirred after the second "Jack" and opened his eyes.

"What's up? What's that sound?"

"Remember the man from Coffee Emporium?"

Jack nodded and Aria continued.

"Well, that same guy is banging on your door right now, and he's been banging on it for at least a minute or two."

"What the hell?" The revelation brought Jack out of his groggy state, and he was climbing out of bed when the knocking stopped. "What do you . . . ?"

Aria cut him off with a whisper. "Hold on a sec. Let's see if he starts up again."

Jack did as he was told but felt ridiculous standing there in his bedroom naked, silently staring at Aria, who was holding her index finger over her lips in the universal "ssshh" command. They both looked silly, so he pulled on his clown pants.

"I'm going to go up." Jack said this in a normal tone, figuring there was no way the man from the coffee shop could hear him from the other side of the door. Aria wasn't so sure, but still fell in behind Jack as he ascended. After waking him up to help her deal with this new, weird situation, she wasn't going to let him go to the door by himself. Besides, she noticed him limping, just a little, as he climbed. He didn't complain about it, had never complained about it as far as she knew, but it made her feel guilty for getting him up. She knew from whence the pain came. It was leftover damage from the accident with Troy.

The knocking was still absent when Jack and Aria reached the top of the steps. He made a face at Aria that indicated he thought the man must have given up but didn't want to say it out loud. Should he still be there, Jack believed he would hear their voices.

Aria motioned Jack to the peephole. She could have looked through it herself but figured she'd be vindicated for the wake-up call if he could simply observe the physical manifestation of the knocker.

Jack put his eyeball to the peephole and was immediately confronted by another eyeball, that of River, who was attempting to use the peephole in reverse. Jack turned away, startled by the vision of River's cornea staring at him from the other side of the magnified tube.

"He's still there." He mouthed the words at Aria, motioning over his shoulder with his thumb.

She whispered back. "What should we do?"

Jack pointed to the steps, making it clear with the gesture he felt they should, quietly but quickly, return to the bedroom. They tip-toed down steps as the banging started up again.

River was sure he'd seen an eyeball on the other side of the aperture, so he started banging on the door again. This was his chance, he told himself, and banged with abandon. If he could just get Jack, and hopefully Aria, to answer the door, he would explain why he was there in the first place. That he wasn't dangerous. That, actually, he was the opposite of dangerous. Well . . . except for the fact that he wanted to expose their suicide cult. But he would make a point not to mention that. In actuality, River had not considered how he was to go about getting this story, vaguely assuming that if he tracked them down, it would just fall into his lap. He never considered they might not want to talk.

After another minute or so of banging, River was forced to conclude that either they were there and avoiding him, or that he was mistaken about the eyeball he thought he'd just seen and no one was home. In any case, he'd reached a point where it no longer mattered. It was cold and snowing, his arm was getting tired, and his knuckles were going to get bloody if he didn't stop. He would have to come up with another strategy.

But what strategy?

River understood he couldn't force anyone to answer a door, and the constant knocking gambit hadn't worked. He had no phone number for the people he believed to be on the other side of the door, and he knew the cops wouldn't give him that information if he asked. He needed a minute to think. He needed a minute to review everything he'd learned since first hearing about Jack and Aria crawling out of the river.

An answer came to him almost immediately. An obvious one. His next best lead was Liberty's Bar and Bottle.

Unbeknownst to River, this was where Jack and Aria's adventure began the day before.

River abandoned his knocking strategy straightaway and walked around the building to the bar. The sign on the door said it would open at 2 o'clock, and River was willing to bet that whoever showed up to open the bar would know at least one of them. He was excited by his heretofore unrecognized powers of deduction.

Now it was a waiting game.

Jack and Aria quietly descended the steps, arriving in the dimly lit bedroom just as the second round of knocking terminated. Like the parents of a newborn that had finally fallen asleep, they were afraid to speak until they were sure the knocking had stopped for good. When the banging did not resume they began to relax, but not completely, and when Jack's body language indicated he was about to speak, Aria again put her index finger to her lips in the silent "sshhh" directive. Jack complied.

They observed a minute of silence.

After that, even Aria was convinced the mysterious door knocker had moved on. Certainly, even a crazed individual wouldn't just hover around the door indefinitely, in inclement weather, waiting for one of them to miraculously exit.

"I think we're okay."

Jack nodded, as if still afraid to speak, even though Aria had already broken their silence.

"I mean, I think we're okay to talk now."

Jack released his breath. "Oh, yeah. Sure."

Aria looked around the room, considering a course of action. Her eyes fell upon the bed, and she smiled, but as much as she wanted to, she wasn't quite ready to consider another attempt at sex. She was still too hyped up from the encounter with the Mad Knocker and told herself that if they were going to remain in the bedroom and not have sex then they may as well try to get some sleep. She was about to mention the idea when Jack spoke up.

"Feel like coffee?"

The question was so random and unexpected that Aria answered without thinking.

"Sure. And, actually, I already made some."

Barring sleep she couldn't honestly think of anything better to do, at least not at the moment. Aria, suddenly excited at the prospect of impressing Jack with her coffee-making skills, also found her interest piqued at the idea of checking on the status of the knocking man.

"Let's just be careful. He still might be out there, lurking."

Jack didn't really buy into her theory but went along with it anyway. For him, the last eighteen hours shattered any number of beliefs he held about how things worked, beliefs he'd largely taken for granted until then. In fact, at that point, as he climbed the steps behind Aria, Jack was willing to reconsider just about anything, even the force of gravity. After all, gravity had been the lynchpin to his whole plan, assuming it would be enough to kill him. It didn't. It didn't kill either of them. That being the case, what other forces in the universe—physical and/or metaphysical—had he misjudged? He silently vowed to keep an open mind to anything.

Aria peeked through the peephole.

She was ninety percent sure no one was hiding on the other side but still felt the need to double-check. The man was gone, at least as far as she could tell through the tiny scope, and his absence left her with an odd sort of confidence, one that convinced her it was safe to move freely about the apartment. Jack watched as Aria and the sweatpants seemed to glide over the wood floor to the coffee, still warm in its heated cradle. He followed in his clown pants, and at that moment, his heart seemed to swell.

It was unexpected, this burgeoning. It stopped him, stopped him from moving. His feet felt trapped, as if buried in the mud of the riverbank. But his eyes still worked, even if his legs didn't, and his eyes were fixed on Aria, her dark hair flowing down her back and the over-large, blue sweatshirt that concealed the contours of her body.

But it was more than the Grinch-like swelling of the heart that took Jack by surprise. Along with it came yearning, yearning of a kind he'd not felt for a very long time, not since before Troy's death. Indeed, it had been so long since Jack had felt anything like it that he wasn't quite sure of the cause.

Am I having a heart attack?

He was not and was quick to recognize that. He was, despite the drinking and generally poor eating habits, in better than average physical condition. Or at least believed himself to be. Regardless, he was much too young for a heart attack.

Panic attack, maybe. His heart was racing. But why would the sight of Aria make him panic?

The answer came involuntarily, like a knee jerk, and the words ballooned from his chest and escaped his mouth before he realized what was happening.

"I think I love you."

The words a whisper, they were now, through no fault of their own, floating around the room amongst the cloud-filtered sunlight and dust particles. Jack wondered what had just happened, but could not put the words back in his mouth, even if he'd wanted to. The swelling feeling, and the yearning that came with it, were symptoms of a long dormant emotional center in his brain, a center suddenly jump-started, as if he'd been tased again. The rush of dopamine and other drugs made him feel all warm and fuzzy. It was much better than the Modafinil, he decided.

At the same time, sadness. The moment reminded Jack of the gut-wrenching pain and heartache that invariably accompanies love. Love in all its forms. So, while part of his brain was unrolling yellow caution tape, telling him to take a minute, another part, the part really connected to the universe, told him everything was going to be okay. It told him this time would be different from all the times before.

And that's the part Jack chose to believe.

As Jack quietly professed his love to Aria, his phone began to ring. He didn't know it was ringing. It was sitting on the nightstand next to the bed, and the sound-deadening qualities of the subterranean bedroom worked in both directions. Sounds less pronounced than a fire alarm were generally unable to clear the steps.

However, even had Jack been in the same room as his phone, and even if he heard it ring, it is still likely the call would have gone unanswered. He would have first looked at the screen to identify the caller, and he would have seen it was his father, who had not spoken to him in nearly a year.

An hour would pass before Jack listened to the voicemail.

Aria heard Jack say the words. She was pouring coffee, augmented with some Kahlua she'd found under the sink, when he said them. The words made her happy. She'd been feeling the same things, but was afraid to express them, lest the feelings not be mutual. She had, after all, sort of glommed onto him the night before, upstaging his suicide attempt by her own fall into the river. They'd been attached at the hip since that moment, and she'd begun to wonder if he actually resented it. Now she knew better, and wondered what took him so long to come to the same conclusion at which she'd arrived hours earlier, at the hospital. She reminded herself that Jack was a man.

"Well, it's about time." She smiled and poured coffee. She almost laughed.

To Aria it all seemed so obvious, with everything they'd been through, everything they'd shared. She wondered how they *couldn't* have fallen in love. She had been feeling this ever since they'd escaped from the river and found themselves huddled on the river bank, trying to protect each other from the wind and snow. Yes, she thought, they'd shared body heat, but also something more.

Until that moment, until the moment she heard the words come out of Jack's mouth, she hadn't questioned why they hadn't come out of hers. Now she did. Now she was forced to admit that waiting for Jack to vocalize the feeling for both of them had been rather cowardly, and she hated to think of herself as a coward. But this was something she couldn't fix, not without a time machine. Jack had said the words first, despite the fact they were barely audible and, therefore, rather half-assed. Certainly, no mountain-top declaration of affection. Still, he got there first. And that fact would be true forever. Now she had to play catch-up.

Aria handed Jack a cup of the enhanced coffee.

"I think I love you too, Jack."

Jack didn't know Aria had heard him, and she took him by surprise, so much so he nearly spit out a mouthful of coffee.

"Um, good coffee. Thanks."

Aria giggled, ignoring the coffee compliment. She teased him.

"Yes, Jack. I heard what you said. You know, when you said you thought you loved me."

Free Will

Aria smiled at Jack's discomfort. His face went a shade redder as he set his mug of Kahlua-laced coffee on the kitchen island.

Jack was between a rock and a hard place, but his choice was simple. He could either attempt an embarrassed retraction, or he could take another step forward toward the terrifying abyss of love that had opened up between them. He chose to step cautiously toward the precipice.

"Well, okay then. I guess *we think* we love each other? No, we do. Yeah. I guess we're in love. So, what do we do now?" Jack paused for a moment. "And, just for the record, I'm sorry that it, 'it' being the event of us falling in love, didn't take place under, you know, *normal* circumstances."

Aria laughed, pulled Jack to her, and kissed him deeply.

"I'm not. I'm not sorry at all. Just think of the great story we get to tell people when they ask us how we got together. Well, I mean, we'll never tell anyone the truth about *why* we were on the bridge. That'd be stupid. But we can lie about that, and then tell the truth about everything that came after, right up until this moment. If you think about it, it's really incredible."

Aria's excitement was infectious, so much so that Jack began to imagine the scenario. He could see it. He could see the two of them having drinks with friends or relatives, telling the story and registering the fear and humor on their faces as they recounted the ordeal in harrowing detail. Of course, he reminded himself, the relatives would have to be Aria's, as most of his family no longer spoke to him. But, still, the vision brought a smile to his face, even as he placed a shadow over it.

"Do you think the lie will come back to haunt us?" he asked. "I mean, don't get me wrong, lying has saved our asses more than a few times in the last twelve hours, but aren't you worried we'll slip up at some point?"

"Nope."

"Okay, but don't you think that, eventually, the truth always comes out? I mean, doesn't the proverbial truth always come out?"

Aria thought about Jack's question. "Nope."

"Really?"

Aria paused. "Well, let's break this down, okay?"

"Okay."

"So, would you agree we have a say in what we do and what happens to us?"

"Yes. Unequivocally. Free will and all that." Jack wasn't yet sure where Aria was going.

"And do you feel the need to tell everyone everything, all the time?"

"Well, no, but . . ."

"And given that no one—meaning none of us, in all of humanity—ever needs to divulge *all* of the things that happen to them, doesn't this mean that we have every right to keep our little secret forever?"

To Jack, Aria's logic seemed nearly unassailable. Why should he have to tell the complete and absolute truth? After all, if confronted with questions about how he and Aria met, he could, quite truthfully, tell them she was the bartender in a watering hole he frequented. Why muddy things with suicidal commentary? It was, he told himself, completely his choice about how he answered that question or, for that matter, any question. The truth, he told himself, could be remarkably nebulous, often open to interpretation. Frustratingly so. Plus, he asked himself, how many people actually wanted to be told everything about everything? How many people, he asked himself, really wanted to hear the whole, frightening story?

No one I know.

Free Will

John refilled his mug, this time more generous with the Kahlua than the last. He enjoyed the effect it was having on his thoughts, already feeling less constricted, less trapped by his behavior over the past year. With each sip, he felt more confident, more assured. He had the power to alter the course of things. He had the power to bring his family back together. He just needed to take the first step. That's all. Just take the first step. After that, the next steps would become obvious.

Chapter Seven

Cleaning and Other Solutions

"So, you like the coffee?"

Aria didn't really need to double-check, but she *did* need to break the silence. After conversing on the philosophical role of truth in humanity, Jack seemed rather stunned. Or, perhaps, just lost in thought. Regardless, she felt the desire to bring him back to her.

"Yeah, absolutely. Is that Kahlua in there? Nice choice."

"I found it under your sink."

"I have no idea how it ended up there. For future reference, there's a liquor cabinet right over there." Jack pointed toward the bookshelves. Aria assumed he was pointing at one of the cabinets on the bottom, the ones with doors on the front, but his finger wasn't overly specific. Should they need more liquor, which was likely, she didn't think she'd have any problems locating whatever they'd need.

"Been a while since you drank it, maybe?"

"Maybe."

Aria sat on the couch, near the fire, and patted the cushion to her left as an invitation for him to sit next to her. He accepted and settled in against her, shoulder to shoulder, and they sipped spiked java in silence, cocooned in the heat radiating from the gas flames. Aria was the first to finish and, after setting her empty mug on the coffee table, threaded her arm through Jack's and rested her head on his shoulder, her eyelids heavy.

"Wow, rationalization is hard work." Her voice was dreamy as her body melted into his. "I think I'm going to try to sleep a little."

"Do you want to lie down on the couch? The fire is nice."

Aria nodded her accord and released Jack's arm so he could stand up and cede the couch to her. From the travel trunk-like coffee table, Jack removed a pillow and blanket and was going to hand them to Aria, but in the time it took Jack to open and close the lid, Aria fully extended herself along the cushions, head resting on her hands, feet at least six inches from the armrest. Jack gently placed the pillow under her head and covered her with the blanket. A moment later she was asleep: exhaustion, Kahlua, and heat from the fireplace overwhelming the caffeine in their battle for supremacy.

Jack envied Aria's ability to fall asleep. He wanted to but was too chemically and emotionally stimulated to find sleep at that moment. Only halfway through his coffee, he wandered to the bookshelves to see if anything caught his fancy. Historically, in similar situations, ones where he needed a distraction, his search generally started on the Vonnegut shelf, but today he decided against it. He'd read and reread the Vonnegut canon in the last year, escaping into it on and off the way he had since a teenager. But at this moment, he didn't feel the need. At this moment, he had his own writing to do.

Where's the log?

Jack, after a cursory search, retrieved it from the nightstand, returned to the kitchen, refilled his mug with coffee and Kahlua, and made a mental note to buy more of the liqueur as soon as was practical, then a second mental note to stop putting it under the sink. He acted on the latter immediately, moving it to the cabinet with the rest of the liquor bottles. Now surrounded by Jack, Jose, Jim, and Evan, the Kahlua looked far happier than it had under the sink. Less lonely.

Jack planted himself in one of the chairs in front of the bookcase, across from the couch.

11:04 AM

Not sure when you'll read this one. Right now you're asleep on the couch.

I'm sitting in a chair across from you.

You've got both hands under your cheek, like a little kid, but don't worry, you're not drooling.

Not yet, anyway.

I've decided not to kill myself. For now, anyway. (Joke)

How, you may ask, did I come to this conclusion?

Hard to say for sure, but I think I'm becoming convinced the universe is trying to send me a message, especially considering my failure to complete the job last night.

And you, of course. You showed up, sort of out of nowhere, to help me.

Like an angel of mercy.

And I don't think we can discount the fact that we both survived a plunge into the river.

I mean, what are the chances?

You'd think at least one of us would have bought it.

So that's why I think the universe wants us to live.

I suppose it's possible there's more to it than that, but I'm still fleshing out the theory.

It's also pretty obvious that the universe wants us to be together. Don't you think?

So, on that note, are you free tonight?

I'm thinking dinner and drinks, but I'm actually up for anything. Clearly.

Maybe just a little sleep first. Maybe not. We'll see how the day goes.

We'll call this our second date. Yup. Easily our second date.

Free Will

Maybe our third? Considering everything we've managed to pack into the last ten or twelve hours, we've definitely got enough material for three dates.
But I won't bug you about it now.
You're sleeping. I'm not going to mess with that.
But maybe when you wake up you can think about it.
I promise we'll stay away from the river and, by extension, any and all bridges.
Unless we're in a car.

Jack stopped and read his log entry, thinking maybe he should tear out the page. Then he changed his mind.

More to come.

Aria was dreaming before Jack tucked the pillow under her head. The Kahlúa was just enough to put her over the edge, just enough to drown the adrenaline she'd produced while the strange man was banging on the front door, the adrenaline she'd produced when Jack told her he was in love with her. Now she was asleep on Jack's couch, feeling as at home as she did in her own apartment. Maybe more so.

Of course, she was *asleep*, and not consciously thinking about how comfortable it was to sleep on Jack's couch. Instead, she dreamt of her dog, the dog she'd received as a present on her seventh birthday. A golden retriever she named Sparky. She'd picked the name Sparky because her friend, Tracy, suggested it was a good name for a dog.

The dream was as long or short as any other dream and, had Aria been conscious, she would have been grateful to have a dream that did not involve her sister. Or, at least partly grateful. Though her dreams of Steffi tended to take dark turns, Aria accepted that as her punishment for not saving her, for not recognizing she needed saving. She deserved them.

She'd done better with Jack. She saw it coming. She saved him.

Jack's cup was empty, so he set the notebook on the coffee table, snatched the Kahlua away from its friends, and went to the kitchen to blend it with more coffee. But now that he accomplished that task, he wasn't sure what his next move should be. He was happy that Aria was getting some sleep but, having finished the log entry he didn't know what to do with himself. He went to the wall of books to see if anything piqued his interest. Under normal circumstances, he would have found any number of books intriguing, but as his eyes swept over the titles, he realized there was no way he could concentrate on some random story. His mind was too full of the last 18 hours, too full of Aria.

What to do? What to do?

From his position by the coffee maker, Jack stared at the couch where Aria was sleeping, silently willing her to wake up. She didn't and, though disappointed with the failure, he didn't find his inability to rouse her with mind power particularly surprising. He'd been trying to bend spoons with his mind since he was a child, when he first saw *The Matrix*, and spent years hoping against hope the latent telekinetic abilities he was sure he had would finally kick in. They hadn't and, as he focused his mental powers on Aria, he wasn't even sure the ability to wake someone up with your mind would even count as telekinesis. In fact, Jack wasn't exactly sure what that particular power would be called.

With nothing better to do, Jack stared, really hard, at the spoon he'd used to stir his coffee. It remained unbent.

He returned to the chair closest to the fire and stared at Aria's face, trying to determine if she was dreaming, and decided it was likely.

From his vantage point he could see her eyelids fluttering, which he was eighty-seven percent sure was a sign of REM sleep. He wondered what she was dreaming about and hoped it was him. He knew this was selfish.

What to do? What to do?

Jack started thinking about therapy, figuring if he was no longer planning to kill himself, it was probably safe to go back to his old shrink, Therapist Jim. Or maybe find a new one. It was now clear to Jack that Therapist Jim's skill set wasn't up to snuff when it came to smoking out a client's hidden, suicidal agenda.

Maybe I'm inscrutable. Or maybe not. After all, Aria figured out what I was up to.

For Jack, however, the biggest problem with switching head doctors was having to start all over again, having to recount the whole thing from the beginning, having to describe, yet again, his relationship with Troy, the evolution of it, and the horrible end of it. Horrible because it always ended with Troy dying. At least Therapist Jim already knew the whole story, he knew every chapter, and there was some comfort in that. The new timeline could start yesterday, and not eight years ago.

But what will I call this new chapter?

Jack decided a good name would be "Suicide Chapter." The Suicide Chapter was very short and had the benefit of a happy ending. So far, anyway.

Still, it was likely Therapist Jim would make him go back in time, further past the moment he started drinking in Liberty's the day before. It was likely Therapist Jim would want to know when his suicidal thoughts began, and why Jack had hidden them from him. This idea, much like the idea of starting with a brand new therapist, seemed every bit as tiresome.

Jack found he was headed down a rabbit hole. It was not hard to recognize. He'd been down this hole before, and it generally took a while to get out, so he decided to change his internal topic of conversation. He needed something to distract himself from his current train of thought, something like alcohol. Or cleaning. Or cleaning *and* alcohol.

Jack recharged his coffee cup, grabbed the duster from under the sink, and started quietly cleaning the bookshelves. It was like magic. Thoughts of painful stories and uncomfortable realities waned with every stroke of the duster. The immediate gratification of cleaning pleased him. It wasn't like his job, at which it could take months or years to get something from the design stage to the actual finished product. In many ways, cleaning was more pleasing than engineering.

Jack finished the bookshelves and was so happy with the results he decided to keep it up, moving on to the lamps and lamp tables, over to the small dry bar and the window sills, until he found himself in the foyer, cleaning the tops of the two paintings. He had half a mind to clean the bathrooms, and within seconds was of a full mind. Jack bounded down the steps to retrieve the appropriate cleaning supplies from the storage closet hiding under the steps.

It was then he heard the ringing.

He could hear the ring, now that he was in the same room as his phone, but decided not to answer it. He was cleaning and drinking, drinking and cleaning, and enjoying it. He was not about to let a cell phone ruin his moving meditation.

But the phone kept ringing. And ringing.

As if the damn thing forgot how to go to voicemail.

Five rings. Six. Was it up to nine?

Jack couldn't take the distraction, abandoned his bucket of cleaning supplies, and grabbed the phone. He didn't recognize the phone number which, had he been following standard protocol, would have resulted in an immediate rejection. But the phone was clearly possessed, or perhaps just broken. In either case it demanded to be answered.

"Hello?"

"Is this Jack?"

"Um, yes, it is. May I ask to whom I'm speaking?"

"This is Lucy Balfour, Aria's mother. Aria called me earlier from your phone, if you recall."

"Yes, of course, Mrs. Balfour. I'm sorry. I just didn't recognize the phone number."

"Well, Jack, I was going to leave a voicemail, but the damn thing wouldn't switch over."

I'm not crazy.

"Yes, I noticed that, too." Jack was smiling, thinking this conversation might turn out to be better than cleaning and drinking, or at least a close second. "What can I do for you?"

"I was just calling to check in on Aria. Would you mind putting her on the phone?"

Jack started to wonder if he could say anything that *didn't* sound like a lie, that *didn't* sound like he was hiding the fact he was a serial killer, and that he hadn't already done Aria in. He figured the best answer was the truth, even if it sounded like a lie.

"I'm sorry, Mrs. Balfour, Aria's sleeping right now. May I take a message?"

May I take a message? Stupid, stupid, stupid. Say something less creepy, dumbass.

"Or I could wake her up if you like."

There you go.

Lucy Balfour paused before speaking. For all Jack knew, she might've silently been instructing her husband to dial 911. "No, Jack, that won't be necessary. But please have her call me when she wakes up."

"You bet. Talk soon."

Jack hung up, deeply questioning the "talk soon" response but convinced the police were not on their way to his house for the second time today. He did not leave the phone on the nightstand, instead dropped it into the oversize pocket of his clown pants. Jack checked the volume of liquid in his coffee cup and estimated, based on current usage, that there remained a ten-minute supply. Just about the perfect amount of time to clean the toilet and sink and throw their dirty river clothes in the wash.

Jack's absence pulled Aria from sleep. Opening her eyes, the first thing that came into focus was the fire. It was the only light in the room other than the thin sunlight forcing its way through the clouds and into the eight-foot windows lining the outside wall. Perfectly relaxed, Aria had no desire to move. She could have stayed in that position indefinitely.

Though she didn't look, Aria was sure Jack wasn't in the room and assumed he was downstairs getting some shuteye. She had the room to herself but, having already explored it, felt no urgency to rouse herself. At least not yet. For now, she could stare at the bookshelves and gauge her level of desire for more coffee and Kahlua or, should the bottle be empty, coffee infused with whatever else Jack had in his liquor cabinet. It didn't take long for the craving to overcome her current state of inertia—brought on by the comfy couch and the warm fire—and she found herself standing in front of the coffee pot, cup in hand. The liqueur sat next to the coffee maker and, luckily, the bottle was not empty.

Though Aria was unaware, in that very moment Jack was on the phone with her mother and, had she known, likely would have intervened. But the acoustic elements of Jack's condo left her blissfully unaware of this new development, and she re-took her seat on the couch, ready to relax until Jack reappeared from the depths. Placing her feet on the coffee table, she stared again at the bookshelves and wondered if there was anything she would enjoy reading. She figured there had to be, given the many and varied volumes laid out before her. She had always enjoyed reading, after all, always loved the escape of it. Perhaps it was time to start reading for pleasure again. She squinted in an attempt to read the titles, but to no avail. They were too far away. But the languor engendered by the couch and the fire had gotten the better of her. The titles would go unread for now.

The notebook was sitting in front of her on the coffee table, so she grabbed it and flipped the pages to Jack's latest entry, smiling as she read the words.

11:23
A date tonight, huh? I'll have to think about it. I'm still pretty sore from our last date.
But what have you got in mind? Shall we go skydiving? Maybe we could go rock climbing in an active volcano. Or we could just stick to bridges, and take our chances. We've already defeated the suspension bridge. It's time to move on to bigger and better things. I agree it's pretty obvious that somehow we're supposed to be together. Fated, even? Maybe. At this point I'm tired enough to believe any theory we come up with. Still, it seems obvious that "forces of nature" have brought us together, and I just wonder what they have in store for us. So, while last night was definitely

exciting, I'm not sure how many more dates like that we can survive. I'm thinking we look for something comparatively lowkey for our next outing. But it occurs to me that, if we could keep all this up, we'd definitely end up with our own reality show. Not sure what we'd call it, though. Aria and Jack Take a Dive? Don't Try This At Home, with Jack and Aria?
50 Ways to Kill Your Lover? I think the possibilities are endless, as long as we survive.
It's nice to hear that you've decided not to kill yourself. That's definitely my preference.
Is it too soon to joke about it?
You're not here to answer that question, but I'm going to assume it's not too soon. I'm going to assume you and I can talk about anything, that we can joke about anything. Even last night. Maybe especially last night. I think, eventually, both of us can move on from the past. We can choose to do that. Together.
I am in love with you, Jack. (Please note that I was the first one to put it in writing. Not that it's a competition.)
Well, listen. I'm sitting on the couch drinking (fortified) coffee, thinking you're downstairs asleep. So I'm going to come down and join you. See you soon.

Aria set the notebook down, headed out of the great room and down the steps. Once downstairs, she was surprised and impressed to find Jack on his hands and knees, cleaning behind the toilet.

"Maybe you could come over to my place and do the same?"

Jack was intensely engrossed in the activity. Startled by Aria's voice, he hit the toilet tank as his head jerked upward.

"Ouch!" Jack, somewhat embarrassed, rubbed the back of his head. "Well, I guess we can add this to our list of cuts and bruises."

"Oh my God, I'm so sorry, Jack. I didn't mean to . . . Are you ok?"

"Absolutely. I think we've proven ourselves to be rather indestructible, don't you think?"

Aria nodded and laughed. "Hell, we might actually be superhuman, but I don't think I'm up for testing that theory, at least not today. Now let me look at your head."

Jack stood but bent over enough for Aria to easily examine the affected area.

"Ooh. You've got a little lump going there. Let me get you some ice."

Jack remembered the phone call before Aria could exit the bathroom.

"Hold on a second. Your mom called. I told her you were asleep, but I'm not sure she bought it."

"Yikes. How did *that* go? I know Mom can be a little intense."

"I think it was fine, other than the part where I thought she might call the cops on me. The faster you call her back the less I have to worry about getting arrested."

Aria took a sip of her drink. "Why would she do that?"

"I don't know. Maybe if she thought I'd killed you or had you chained to a wall."

Aria laughed. "Sounds like I should call her right away. I think we've had enough of the police for one day."

Jack handed his phone to Aria. Her mother answered on the first ring.

"Hi Mom. It's me."

"No, I'm good. I was sleeping when you called and talked to Jack."

"No, I'm fine. He's really nice." Aria smiled at Jack and put her hand on his cheek to emphasize his niceness.

"Yes. Just waiting for Tracy to get here with my keys so I can get back into my apartment."

"No, Mom. I already showered. I don't need another one."

"Yes. I showered here." Aria lowered her hand to Jack's chest, making his skin tingle.

"No. We didn't shower together. I've got to let you go, Mom."

"Because I've got to go to the bathroom and I don't want to talk on the phone while I'm, you know, *going* to the bathroom."

"That's very nice of you, Mom. I'll ask him and let you know."

"Yes. I will ask him."

"I will. I promise. Talk to you later."

Aria handed the phone to Jack. "Feel like having a cocktail with my parents later?"

Jack was saved from answering by a knock on the door.

John knew what he needed to do first, and found Susan sitting on the lounger in their bedroom, reading a book. "I'm going to ask Jack to come over tonight. And I'm going to invite the family. You can be part of it, or don't, but either way, I'm making the call." He waited for a moment but received no response from his wife beyond a confused stare. John went back to the kitchen and dialed the phone.

Chapter Eight

An Unexpected Guest

Jack traveled, as silently as possible, to the door to peer through the peephole, expecting to find the Mad Knocker at it again. Instead, there was a young woman on the other side; he did not recognize her.

Jack pulled his head back from the door to look down at Aria who, curious, had sidled up next to him.

"It's some girl. Not sure who she is." He whispered the words, a cautionary tactic left over from earlier that morning. "Wanna take a look?"

Aria stood on tiptoes, trying to get a good view, and immediately recognized their newest visitor.

"It's Tracy!"

"Who?"

"My friend, Tracy. You know, the one who has my phone? The one we are supposed to meet at Liberty's at 2? The one who gave me her coat?" Aria whispered as well, as if she feared her friend would hear her from the other side of the door.

"Ah, of course. Tracy."

Before they could consult further, Jack opened the door to reveal Tracy standing in the snow, one hand cocked, ready to give the door another rap with her fist.

"Hi, Tracy. I'm Jack." Jack extended a hand from his side of the threshold while Aria, half hidden by Jack's body, gave Tracy a short wave.

Surprised by the stranger greeting her, Tracy took a moment to gather herself before taking Jack's hand in hers. Even then, even as she shook his hand, she could hardly believe the man named Jack was actually standing before her, in the flesh. She'd gone to bed the night before, secure in the knowledge that Aria had not given her the full story on Jack, but also that she was truly frightened for him.

"Ah, the mythical Jack. I'm amazed. I'll be honest, I wasn't sure you actually existed. I thought my friend there, the one hiding behind you, might have just been having an episode."

"Please, come in."

Tracy released Jack's hand and stepped through the doorway into the foyer. She was as smartly dressed as she'd been the night before but was now carrying a large shopping bag.

"Can I take that for you?"

Though she was in the process of receiving a hug from Aria, Tracy still managed to extend the bag to Jack, who dutifully relieved her of her burden and set it gently on the floor in the corner of the foyer.

Aria kept the hug going until she was sure she'd transmitted the requisite amount of love and gratitude. Aria kept the hug going until she felt her eyes fill with tears.

"What are you doing here? I thought we weren't going to meet up until 2 o'clock, you know, in Liberty's."

"I had to come down here anyway. I think I left my credit card over at that bar we were at last night. Kaze, right? Anyway, I couldn't get in there until lunch and I figured I might as well combine trips. Your coat, phone, and keys are in the bag. The phone seems to be working. It's on, anyway."

"Thank you! But how did you know where Jack lives?"

Given the exponentially high number of unexpected guests that morning, Jack was wondering the same thing, although his curiosity was largely intellectual. He had no intention of getting involved in their conversation, nor was he concerned about the means by which Tracy obtained his home address. Jack was content that Aria's things had been recovered, that they could now access her apartment and, by extension, her wardrobe, though he doubted there was anything in her closet quite as alluring as the sweats she was currently wearing.

Tracy gave Aria's shoulder a playful shove. "Dummy, we were in Liberty's last night. You told me he lived in the same building as the bar. Remember? I wasn't sure which door, though, so I tried this one and got lucky."

Aria's face turned a bright pink. She'd forgotten that little piece of information and was embarrassed to have it revealed in front of Jack. Now she wondered if he thought her obsessed, perhaps pining for him as she worked through a hopelessly unrequited love. Or perhaps a stalker.

Wait! Am I obsessed with Jack? How long have I loved him? Is that what this is? Or is it just a crush? Is there a difference?

Aria tried to walk herself back from her internal discourse on the nature of her feelings for Jack and turned her head, ever so slightly, in his direction, attempting to gauge his reaction to Tracy's revelation. As far as she could tell, the comment had not registered, or perhaps he'd just not heard it. Or, in the worst-case scenario, he heard Tracy's comment and was now mulling it over in his head, trying to figure out if it meant anything to him and, if so, what that might be. Or if it meant nothing at all. She grabbed one more clandestine look at Jack. Nothing registered. As she started to relax her face returned to its natural color, but she realized she needed to change the topic as quickly as possible.

"Anybody want mimosas?"

Tracy looked surprised. "Really? You've decided *now* is a good time for mimosas?"

Jack laughed out loud at Tracy's reaction. He felt it was, indeed, the perfect time for mimosas, and was already taking silent inventory to make sure he had the requisite ingredients of orange juice and prosecco. He had both, he determined, but hoped no one suggested they put together a charcuterie or some other iteration of finger food. His suicide plan had purposely not included restocking the perishables before killing himself. He did, however, have plenty of alcohol, figuring liquor would easily last until the funeral, where it could be deployed as needed. The orange juice was a selfish choice. It accompanied the Wheat Chex he consumed almost every morning and he wasn't going to deny himself his favorite breakfast on his last day among the living.

Though Jack said nothing, he had, in fact, taken note of Tracy's revelation that the two of them, at Aria's exhortation, had performed a walk-by of his condo the night before. It didn't bother him, and actually made him feel closer to her. Until then he'd not put much thought into the idea of a guardian angel, but was now convinced that if they existed, his was named Aria. He only hoped that someday he could be the same for her, though perhaps in somewhat less dramatic fashion.

Aria, desperate to move the conversation forward, broke into Jack's reverie.

"Jack, do you have what it takes?"

Jack nodded as the question, an unintentional double entendre, took him by surprise. Suddenly, he wasn't at all sure he had "what it takes," at least not in any category beyond the availability of mimosa ingredients. He was confident he had those; it was everything else of which he was unsure. Everything else. After all, he hadn't intended to make it to this day; did not figure he'd ever again be confronted with these types of questions, even by accident. His life, until just a few hours ago, had an expiration date, and now here he was, confronted with the reality of his own, unplanned existence. He found it all a bit jarring.

What to do? What to do?

Tracy's voice yanked him from the abrupt philosophical nose dive.

"Well, I suppose if you two are having one . . ." Tracy could smell the freshly brewed coffee and considered asking for a cup but felt the request would ruin the spirit of the moment.

"Great. Great. I'll get things started. Jack, can you point me to the prosecco?"

Tracy had more errands to run, but her fascination with the performance playing out in front of her made it impossible to walk away. She had so many questions, but was afraid she might begin stepping on emotional toes should she leap too quickly into an interrogation. In the meantime they could all relax with a drink and, when the relaxing advanced to the inevitable drink number two, she was sure to find an opportunity to drill into the mystery of Aria and Jack.

"Nice outfits by the way. I didn't know 'clown' and 'locker room' were the new black."

Tracy giggled, but her comment reminded them that she had no idea what had happened to them in the time since she'd traded coats with Aria. Not a clue.

Aria, searching Jack's cabinets for appropriate mimosa glassware, found herself in a bit of a panic, wondering if she should come clean or, instead, try to make up a story plausible enough for her best friend to believe. She glanced at Jack, his eyes pleading. She wasn't sure, but suspected the pleading to be along the lines of "Please say something before I have to," but Aria couldn't say anything. Her brain was in overdrive, one thought crowding out another, washing out any words that might have made sense at the moment. Jack saved the day with a surprising dose of truth, albeit not the whole truth, about their state of dress.

"I was going to put our clothes from last night in the wash so, you know, this is what I had available and, seeing as Aria couldn't get into her apartment and all, this is the best we could do. Well, until now anyway, now that you brought the keys."

Tracy heard Jack's explanation and now, like Aria, found herself dumbstruck. So much information was transmitted in Jack's short sentence that she needed a minute to formulate the questions the statement inspired. Those questions ran the gamut, but mostly posed some version of "You two spent the night together? How did that happen?" She tried to pull it together.

"Well, of course you wouldn't have anything to fit her."

Jack kept going, distracting Tracy further.

"And, you know, since she looked ridiculous, she thought it was only fair that I look ridiculous as well, so I've been running around in these all morning." Jack made a sweeping gesture over his polka-dotted pants.

"Running around? You've been running around in clown pants? Outside? Where people can see you?"

Aria shook her head, thrilled that Jack willingly stepped into the metaphorical minefield to distract Tracy, and with the truth, no less. Now she felt ready to shoulder some of the burden.

"Just Coffee Emporium. And back, of course. I mean, we're not crazy, if that's what you're thinking. Is that what you're thinking? That we're crazy? Honestly, these clothes are temporary, we only planned to wear them until I could get into my apartment. And now I can, because you've saved the day. Again." The baggy sweatshirt flopped around as Aria motioned excitedly with her hands.

Tracy had no idea what was happening. Everything was moving fast. Her head was swimming. It wasn't that she hadn't received a sensible explanation for Jack's and Aria's off-beat style choices. She had.

It was everything that *wasn't* being answered. All the questions she wanted to ask, and all the questions she didn't know she wanted to ask. Clearly, a lot had happened since she'd last seen her friend the night before.

"Well, that's . . . good, then. I'm glad I can be of service." Tracy found some footing. "But, you know, I have a lot of questions about . . . about last night, if you don't mind me asking."

Aria finished her mimosa-making before Tracy had time to further inquire "about last night," and distributed the full glasses before addressing Jack.

"Can I pull you aside for a minute?"

Without waiting for an answer, and giving Tracy an apologetic half-smile, Aria took Jack by the elbow, led him out of the kitchen and down the steps to the bedroom. Given Tracy's bumbling attempts to discern the "story behind the story," Jack was not surprised by Aria's desire to speak discreetly and did not resist her, even managing to take a few sips of the mimosa on their way down the steps.

"What's up?" Jack took another sip of the mimosa.

"What do we do with Tracy?"

"What do you mean? Do you think we need to get rid of her? And by that I mean kill her." Jack kept a straight face.

"Yeah, funny." Aria punched him in the shoulder, nearly causing Jack to spill some of his drink. "Well, yes. I guess get rid of her. But I don't want to be mean or anything like that."

"Got it. No killing." Jack thought for a moment. "Can you tell her we have to run over to your house? Would that sound too obvious? I mean, I don't think it's cool to just tell her she has to leave, especially not after she made a special trip to bring you your stuff. On the other hand, I think we're being really nice about the 'not killing' so, on balance . . ."

"Ok. Still not funny and no, we can't just tell her to leave. I've known her since we were kids. She's up there trying to put two and two together and we're not going to be able to deflect much longer. Either we come up with a good reason to leave your condo or . . . or we just go ahead and tell her the truth."

The prospect of expanding their tiny truth circle did not please Jack. Though he believed in the basic efficacy of the truth setting one free, he also believed that, in this case, telling the truth was bad. He told himself the circumstances under which he was operating the night before, the suicidal circumstances, were old news. He was sure everything had changed since they went off the bridge and he no longer had any desire to off himself. Well, at least he didn't think he did. He was sure he could handle the residual and, that being the case, felt it unnecessary to rehash the whole evening or, for that matter, the whole year that led up to it. He took a sip of mimosa and tried to be witty without being dismissive.

"The truth? What if she can't handle the truth?"

"She's going to have to." Aria ignored the joke and took Jack's mimosa-free hand into her mimosa-free hand. "Listen, Jack. Trust me when I tell you she's not going to let this go. We may get her to leave for now, but I'll bet a billion dollars she'll call me on my rice-dried cell phone as soon as she gets in her car and pump me for information until she's satisfied that what I'm telling her is the truth."

"I don't believe you actually have a billion dollars."

Aria paused to squeeze Jack's hand.

"I know you want to keep all this . . . you know . . . on the down low, and I wouldn't push for the truth thing if I didn't think we could trust her to keep it to herself. Plus, she already has a clue. When I saw her last night, I had to tell her why I was looking for you."

That Tracy already knew what Jack was up to the night before was news to him. "What did you tell her?"

"Just that I was afraid you were going to hurt yourself and that I wanted to stop you."

"Wow. Well, that's pretty much it then, isn't it?"

"Well, sort of. She doesn't know we ended up in the river or, for that matter, anything that happened until she got here this morning."

"Okay. Well, I guess we might as well come clean. In for a penny, in for a dollar, or a pound, or whatever."

Jack wasn't completely convinced by his own argument. Yes, he told himself, he wasn't sure he was ready to let the world in, to have himself exposed to its cruelties just because he felt a need to come clean. He'd spent a year cultivating his inner hermit, spent a year building a cocoon. He was not thrilled with the idea of stripping away that layer of protection. At least not this way. Like ripping off a Band-Aid. His death was meant to save him from the pain of killing his nephew. Now his inability to stop living had become problematic, but there was no longer any point in hiding from Tracy. He'd been drained of the energy needed to maintain the subterfuge.

"Ok. I think it's fine. Let's tell her the truth. I trust you to know what to do."

Aria was surprised to feel a bit deflated by Jack's easy acquiescence. Whilst making mimosas, she'd spent at least a minute preparing what she believed was a convincing argument for the truth, at least convincing enough to sway Jack. Part of her was disappointed that he caved so easily, but only because it denied her the opportunity to present her lawyerly justification. Nonetheless, she recovered quickly.

"Well, okay then. I'm glad you feel that way." Aria said nothing of her well-structured, debate-ready rebuttal to Jack's initial reaction to the let's-all-tell-the-truth idea. "I say we head back upstairs and answer her questions. Besides, I'm out of mimosa."

Jack looked down at the dwindling contents of his own glass. "Yeah, I'm running low as well. But, Aria, one last time: are you sure she can keep secrets?"

"She's kept all of mine."

That was enough for Jack, even as he wondered what Aria's secrets might be. He followed her up the steps, noting with some amusement that the sweats seemed to have gotten even baggier than when she'd first donned them. This did not stop him from remembering what was underneath.

Tracy watched Aria and Jack disappear down the steps. Her Sensible Self told her to stay put until they returned, but her Curious Self easily won the moment. She was desperate to understand everything the newly-minted couple had been telling her and felt the need to eavesdrop. Despite the thickness of her snow boots, Tracy managed a half-assed tiptoe to the top of the steps and was disappointed when all she could hear were muffled voices rising to her from below, voices that sounded like they were being filtered through thick blankets.

Feeling exposed in the foyer, and afraid to be caught snooping, Tracy carefully tiptoed back to her starting position at the kitchen island. With nothing better to do, she went ahead and poured a glass of orange juice and prosecco and, drink in hand, waited for Aria and Jack to ascend.

Aria noticed the drink in Tracy's hand as she entered the kitchen, silently hoping there were enough ingredients to make at least two more, and for this she felt guilty. She and Jack were about to spill their guts. Now was not the time to be so easily distracted by thoughts of another mimosa, no matter how tasty it might be. In fact, she was ninety-eight percent positive that these were the best mimosas she'd ever consumed. She also believed the exquisite flavor of the drinks themselves was likely a direct result of having cheated death some twelve hours earlier, and that her near-death experience was magnifying everything. She'd noticed it earlier, this magnification, when she was with Jack or drinking a Kahlua and coffee. Even sleeping on the couch. Everything was better than it had ever been; everything was . . . *more.*

Aria pulled herself together. She had more important things to worry about than if mimosas would ever taste this good again. Still, she was relieved Jack poured two more. Clearly, they had yet to exhaust the supply of ingredients.

Fishes and loaves.

"So, Tracy. I know you're probably a little confused by all this." Aria swept her hands over her and Jack's baggy garments.

"That's putting it lightly."

"Well, we were talking downstairs, obviously, and we decided to tell you the truth about what happened to us last night, and to answer any questions you want to ask."

Tracy took a sip of her drink. "Oh, please, do tell. Can't wait to hear it." She plopped down in a chair and the couple took the couch opposite. The fire still burned cheerily, in defiance of the dreary winter light, illuminating Jack and Aria's faces.

Aria ignored her friend's sarcasm and launched into the story, starting with the moment Tracy drove away, just after they traded coats. Aria relayed the details of her journey but took a break every few sentences to give Jack a chance to fill in the details of his own. When Aria spoke of talking to the police in front of the Main Event, Jack took his turn to fill them in on the details of the bar fight and how he managed to escape Kevin, his temporary sidekick, in order to make his way to the bridge alone. She spoke of seeing and talking to her ex-boyfriend, Brian, in the Bay Horse saloon while Jack told of having what he thought would be his last drink ever in the same bar just a few minutes before Aria arrived.

Aria and Jack found their back-and-forth dissertation on the events of the night before as informative as did Tracy. They realized that, despite the intensity of the time they'd spent together, they'd not used any of that time to fully debrief one another on the twists and turns of their respective evenings.

Of course, it was at the bridge where their stories merged, and it was with the merging that the pace of the story sped up. Then each had something to say about the other, as if a ping-pong ball were bouncing between them and each bounce resulted in new information. Jack and Aria laid everything on the table; nothing was omitted. Tracy listened, enthralled by the story of their escape from the river, huddling for warmth, Jack getting tased, and the loss of the original notebook. She listened intently to the tale of their ambulance ride with a drunken priest, psych tests, evasion of Deputy Lane, stolen drugs, and sex in a storage closet. Tracy did her best to keep up and did not interrupt, but was sure she still wasn't catching everything, the recounting coming so quickly.

By the time they finished, Aria was exhausted, unsure if the exhaustion was from lack of sleep combined with more alcohol, or a result of the great unburdening she and Jack had just undertaken. Regardless, she was ready for a nap, or perhaps another mimosa. Tracy's voice interrupted her contemplation.

"Wow. Okay, guys. That's a lot. I mean, really, that's a lot. Do you even realize how much this is? How big it is? I mean, really. It's so much . . . so hard to believe. But, you know, lucky to be alive, and all that. It's just . . . a lot. I don't really know what to say. I mean, it sounds more like a book than real life. It'll take me a while to process it. And, speaking of processing, how the hell have you guys managed to cope with all this?"

Aria and Jack laughed, but not at Tracy. They laughed at the question; they laughed at each other.

Aria answered for both of them.

"Sex, drugs, and the occasional nap."

John left a message and hung up. The message was simple, boiled down. He wanted to mend the fence. John slumped in his chair at the kitchen island. He felt exhausted, exhausted by the death of his grandson, exhausted by the effort to cut his son out of his life. All the effort had sucked the life out of him and his family and it had to stop. So he left the message and waited.

Chapter Nine

Miles to go before I sleep

Tracy couldn't help but laugh. The gravity of the story was not lost on her but she had no helpful response. She was pleased, however, to learn that her intervention the prior evening had actually done some good, though her winter coat would never be the same, no matter how many trips it made to the dry cleaner. It had survived, but not unscathed. As well, the trading of coats had saved Aria's phone from a watery demise, and Tracy smiled at the unforeseen results of her act of kindness. But now she had something else on her mind.

"Hey, not to go too far off-topic, but your mother invited me and Richard over for drinks later. She said you and 'your new friend' would be there."

"She did?" Aria was considering adding another splash of prosecco to her glass.

"Yep. Already got a babysitter."

Aria laughed at Tracy's ability to switch so easily to thoughts of a cocktail party right after being regaled with the "Adventures of Jack and Aria."

But Aria had something more important to discuss.

"So, Tracy, my best friend, my confidant. Can you keep all this just between us? Even if you're drinking at my house? Especially when you now have the best happy hour story ever, can you keep from telling it?"

Tracy felt a tad offended, wondering why Aria felt the need to ask the question at all. After all, they'd been friends for nearly twenty years. They knew everything about each other. They'd kept so many secrets that most had been forgotten. Still, part of her could see Aria's point. The tale of her friend's adventures was the epitome of out-of-the-ordinary and, if divulged, would surely make the storyteller the life of the party. But it would never be worth the betrayal.

"C'mon! Do you think things are going to change between us because you got arrested for not knowing how to walk across a bridge? What kind of friend would that make me?"

Struck by her own stupidity, Aria was abruptly reminded she'd known the answer to her question before she asked it.

"Yes, stupid question. Absolutely. Sorry I asked, Tracy."

But there was something, a small something, nagging at Aria.

"Ok, just for the record, you know, we weren't arrested, at least not officially." Aria paused. "Well, at least I don't think so. Jack?"

Jack replayed the last twelve hours as fast as the mimosas and exhaustion would allow. In succession, his memory called forth Sergeant Thompson, Deputy Lane, all the paramedics, the doctors and nurses, the pharmacist, and the janitor who nearly caught them having sex in a supply closet. He remembered the blood tests, the suicide test, and the psych referral that never came to fruition. But nothing in the replay had them getting arrested, at least not officially, and Jack was eighty-nine percent sure an official arrest would have been accompanied by the cuffing of wrists and reading of Miranda rights. He did not recall such a reading, though it was certainly possible the tasing administered by Deputy Lane took out a brain cell or two.

"Nope. I don't think we were ever arrested. I don't even remember getting handcuffed, even after I was electrocuted."

"You got electrocuted?" Tracy turned to Aria. "How did you miss that little tidbit?"

Aria smiled. "I didn't miss it. He's talking about getting tased. I think he's just being dramatic."

Jack didn't think using the word "electrocuted" after getting struck with 50,000 volts of electricity by an unreasonably aggressive deputy sheriff was overly "dramatic," but understood he was being teased. Now, however, he was faced with a creeping concern that his confrontation with the mini lightning bolt may well be responsible for a partial memory loss, a loss he was not at all certain was temporary. But Jack took comfort in the idea that the memory loss, if there was any, was likely due to the impromptu electro-shock therapy rather than a side effect of the alcohol and drugs they'd consumed. He preferred to believe that any brain damage had been suffered at the hands of something over which he had no control.

Tracy continued to pepper Jack and Aria with questions, doing her best to glean the details missed during the initial, rapid-fire telling of the story. Aria was happy to oblige, but Jack was experiencing another wave of exhaustion and was, as a result, losing enthusiasm for this round of question and answer. It was in the middle of one of Tracy's questions, something about how river water tasted and how much did they accidentally drink, that Jack's phone vibrated. He used his buzzing clown pants as an excuse to avert his attention from Aria and Tracy.

A cursory examination made it clear the reason for the buzz was a spam text extolling the benefits of day trading and how one could become rich if they were only willing to spend $49.95. Jack couldn't hit the delete button fast enough, and once the phone was back on the home screen he noticed something else—a missed call and voicemail from a number he'd memorized when he was ten. It was his father.

Jack was struck dumb. The last conversation he'd had with John Current occurred six weeks after the accident, when his father picked him up from physical therapy. Although Jack was able to drive, at times he found it terrifying. Outside of his shrink, he hadn't told anyone this, but until then hadn't needed to.

"Listen, Jack. You're able to get to physical therapy on your own, right?"

Jack detected a tone in his father's voice, a voice that had always been confident and strong, but now sounded unsure. Even ashamed.

"Well, yeah, Dad." Jack shifted in his seat to try to get his hip to stop aching, but his father was making him even more uncomfortable. "Why? What's going on?"

John paused. He was about to have a difficult conversation with his second son, a conversation he didn't want to have, but had been cowed into having. He still wasn't sure why he'd agreed to have the conversation, other than an attempt to make the women in his life a little less unhappy. Maybe that was enough.

John's voice choked. "The thing is, Jack . . . Well, the thing is that there's a lot of anger."

Jack understood where his father was going and decided to relieve him of his misery. "It's okay, Dad. I understand. I'll figure it out."

Jack did understand. He'd seen the breach coming weeks before, during the last conversation with his mother, one in which she'd broken down and told him she was doing her best not to hate him, that she would need time, and that she couldn't see him, not for a while. The tears in his father's eyes spoke volumes. Jack had destroyed his family.

Jack's brain cruelly replayed that day, the first time he'd ever seen his father cry. He hadn't seen his father's number pop up on his phone since, nor his mother's, or his brother's, so Jack could be excused for momentarily zoning out of the conversation with Aria and Tracy. A few moments later, after the memory was released, Jack looked up to find Aria staring at him.

"Are you okay?"

"Um, yeah, I'm good . . . I think my dad left me a message this morning."

It was Aria's turn to be stunned. In the last year, and especially in the last day, she'd come to understand the split between Jack and his family. She knew what had to happen next.

"Tracy. Time to go."

Aria covered the two steps between her and Tracy. She took the drink from Tracy's hand, grabbed her coat off a hook and thrust it into her arms, all before Tracy realized what was happening.

"What? Why? What's going on?"

Aria already had her halfway to the front door. "I'll explain later. I'll call you. Or maybe I'll see you at my parents."

"Oh, well, damn, Aria." Tracy protested as Aria pushed her out into the snow. "Alright, alright. I'm out. Jeez. I'll talk to you later."

Aria closed the door.

River Van Beek was frustrated. He'd spent his entire morning chasing down what he believed to be a huge story and came up with next to nothing. Now he was sitting in yet another coffee shop, one clearly owned and operated by hippies, right across the street from Liberty's Bar and Bottle. Other than a core belief that they didn't regularly bathe, River had no problem with hippies. Evidence to support his theory on their personal hygiene was anecdotal and reinforced by the generally unkempt appearance favored by the hippie subgroup, but River figured if you didn't look like you'd showered that morning, you probably hadn't. He believed this even if he detected no discernible body odor, so he was not particularly pleased to be drinking coffee in a hippie coffee shop, even if he found the coffee quite tasty. The advantage to this coffee house, of course, was that it provided him a clear line of sight to the door he believed was owned by one of the "swimmers." From his table he would see anyone enter or leave the premises. Plus, the shop was nice and cozy.

River took a sip of coffee and gave the place a once-over, noting that although the employees were hippies, the customers they were serving were mostly hipsters, a different breed altogether, and easily discernible from hippies by their favored beanie hats, neck scarves, and skinny jeans that were generally two or three inches too short. River didn't mind hipsters so much, even if he wasn't a fan of the short, long pants.

Dressed, as he was, in a loose-fitting brown suit, white shirt, and brown leather oxfords, River didn't fit in with the noontime clientele and was well aware of this fact. But he felt he had no choice but to endure, no choice but to sit and wait. He'd believed the intelligence gleaned at Coffee Emporium would be enough to track down the swimmers and regrouped when that didn't pan out. He now found himself lying in wait, hoping the objects of his quest would miraculously appear.

River thought about asking the other patrons about Jack and Aria, but felt the need to fortify himself, just a little, before undertaking such a task. Unlike Coffee Emporium, this shop was small, offering no privacy to go about his business, so instead he sat and procrastinated, quietly sipping coffee and nibbling on a pastry, one eye on the street in front of Jack's condo and one eye on his solitaire app. It was then, in a moment he could only describe as a gift from above, he spied a well-dressed woman nearly fall out of the condominium door, the one on which he'd been savagely knocking not so long ago. Surprised, River burned his lips with the hot coffee and only partially contained his spit-take. He snapped a quick pic with his camera.

I got you now.

Jack heard the door shut and the lock being set. A second later Aria was standing in front of him.

"Are you okay?"

"Um, I think so. Maybe? It's just that, you know, I haven't talked to any of them for almost a year."

"You have to listen to the message."

Jack wasn't sure he *had* to listen to the message, but understood he *would* listen to it, despite the words that might be in it. He just didn't know when. They might be good words, or bad, but either way he wasn't convinced he wanted to hear them yet, because no matter what the words might be, they were going to upset his apple cart. And over the last year he'd worked hard to organize his cart. The events of the last twenty hours had already jumbled everything up, and he was positive his father's message would only add to the jumbling.

"Jack, do you want me to leave while you listen to it? Would that help?" Aria was sure whatever was in the message was big. Really big. John Current wasn't calling just to say hello.

Jack stared at Aria. "No, it's okay. I don't think I'm going to listen to it right away. It's fine."

Aria wondered if Jack was in shock; she wondered if she was in shock. She was surprised at how surprised *she* was by the call, by how anxious she felt for Jack.

"Ok, how about this? If you want, I'll listen to the message first, and then, you know, give you sort of a summary, and then you can decide if you want to listen to it or not."

Jack did not find Aria's proposal unreasonable, even given his current state of mind, and said so as he handed Aria his phone, which she took to the spare bedroom, closing the door behind her. She emerged less than a minute later, tears in her eyes as she handed Jack his phone.

"You should listen. Really. It's good."

Still in a stupor, his resistance subsided, Jack played the message.

Free Will

"Jack, it's your father. I want to see you. I mean we want to see you. This has been terrible, this situation. A terrible year. And I've been terrible and this has to stop. We need to be a family again. It's not your fault that we haven't been. It's ours. It's mine. Please call me. I know you may not want to. I know that you are hurt. You have every right to be. But please call me. I'm here and I'm not going anywhere. I love you."

Jack stepped to the couch and lowered himself onto it. Aria sat down next to him and took his hand in hers. She said nothing. There was nothing to be said. She didn't want to interrupt Jack's thoughts, his processing of the message from his father. He needed space, at least for now.

His voice startled her.

"I think I want to lie down."

Jack stood up and walked toward the stairs, his limp a little more noticeable than it had been since they left the hospital, adding an authentic touch to his zombie-like shuffle. Aria stayed put, figuring now might not be the time to join him in bed. Besides, she could use the time to make more coffee, or call Tracy to explain why she shoved her out into the cold without warning, but instead of doing either of those things she grabbed the notebook and started writing.

12:14

Jeez, Jack. Could today get any more dramatic? I mean that in the best way. I mean, hearing from your family? Today? After . . . last night? I swear, sometimes I really do believe the universe has a plan. In this case a plan for you, specifically. Even as I write this, I wonder how we managed not to die last night, and what we would have missed if we had. Think about it. You wouldn't ever have gotten that call from your father. It would have arrived just hours too late. Or, and not to sound morbid, had you been successful last night he may have never had the chance to make the call. He probably would have found out what happened before he ever picked up the phone. Honestly, my head is swimming with this stuff.

I'm thinking, more and more, that all this is more than luck. I know, I know. I'm probably just blowing smoke, but it's hard to deny the outcome of, you know, everything. I mean, if it didn't all happen to me, to us, I never would have believed it. So what do we do with this gift we've been given?

Oooh. That was heavy, wasn't it? But, seriously, we should think about that. Maybe not today. I think we've got enough on our plate for today. Later, though. After things calm down a bit. We've got a lot to learn about each other in the meantime.

On a less ominous note, I need to run home and get some clothes. No matter what we end up doing later (not to sound too assuming). I know our clothes from yesterday are clean now, but I'm going to need more stuff for the day, stuff that's in my apartment.

Aria slid the pen back into the wire binding and wondered if she should invite Jack to go with her to her apartment. She decided she should. She wasn't ready to leave him alone. In fact, she was actually afraid to leave him alone, unsure if he was really out of the woods with the whole suicide thing. Besides, she figured, they could both use a little movement.

Setting the notebook back on the coffee table, she descended the steps to Jack's bedroom. The nightstand light still burned, allowing her to see around the room. Jack lay on his side, turned away from her, but she could hear his breathing. He must have dozed off in the short time they'd been separated.

Almost on a whim, Aria rejected her earlier position on joining Jack in bed and slipped in under the covers, pulled herself to him until they were spooning, and placed her arm over his chest. For the moment, the thought of running to her apartment for clothes and makeup faded. When the pressure of her body against his brought Jack to the waking world, he rolled around and drew her tighter against him. This seemingly small gesture released a geyser of emotion that had been building in Jack and Aria over the last 20 hours. The sex was immediate and intense, their foreplay an explosion of bedcovers and clothing as they hurdled toward a melding of hearts and flesh. This time, impervious to distractions, they felt no pain from their wounds. Each ached to crawl into the other, unable to get close enough, longing to find that place of unqualified acceptance, of peace, of forgiveness.

Afterwards, came the tears—tears of relief, of gratitude, of possibility. Everything was . . . *more*.

The emotional release and physical exertion sapped what little energy they'd stored since leaving the hospital that morning. Jack dozed again, but not for long. Now, he spooned Aria and could feel her chest expand and contract, her breathing shallow as she drifted off. Happy she'd fallen asleep, he began to doze, but something jerked him awake and he knew he wouldn't go back to sleep until he did something about it. Ever so gently, he unwrapped himself from Aria, slipped out of bed, pulled on the clown pants and baggy shirt, and mounted the steps.

It was still cloudy, but now the clouds seemed ominous, oppressive. Jack hoped Aria had made more coffee, but not because he thought he needed it to stay awake. He needed something warm in his stomach so, upon finding the pot empty, started a new batch. The glass carafe was spotless.

Thanks, Aria. That was very nice of you.

Jack paced the great room while the coffee brewed, touching items in his path as if he'd never seen them before. The room seemed different from what he remembered, or at least different from the day before. It was warmer than yesterday. The room felt *cozier*, a trait Jack had never before ascribed to his condominium, no matter how comfortable he'd been in the space. Now, however, his comfort seemed . . . *enhanced*.

Too impatient to wait for the machine to brew the entire pot, Jack held on just long enough to fill his mug, setting the carafe back in the machine before taking a seat on the couch. In front of him, on the coffee table, was the notebook. He opened it to Aria's last entry and composed his response.

John Current was nervous. He'd moved back and forth from the kitchen island to the couch in the family room at least five times while he waited for the phone to ring, waited for his son to call him back. The conversation with Susan had been difficult, but brief and to the point, and now that he had that out of the way he only felt the need to hear his son's voice again, to know that he'd gotten the message.

Chapter Ten

Hoarders Among Us

12:31 PM
Drama? That's putting it lightly. I can't think of a time like this. Ever.
Of course, I realize that I caused all this. Even your part. Even Dad's part.
If it hadn't been for the accident with Troy . . . If it hadn't been for me, you know . . .
trying to kill myself, well, then none of this would have happened.
So, I suppose, in a twisted way, I'm happy I tried to kill myself, and that I was NOT successful.
Wow, it really is a lot to think about. My head is swimming also.
I'm afraid to call my father. So much has happened in the last year, since the last time
I talked to him. I didn't blame him then, and I don't blame him now.
But what if what he's feeling is only temporary? Will he change his mind tomorrow?
Will my mom? Speaking of which, he didn't say anything about her. Mom, I mean.
I suspect she and Sarah (Troy's mother and my brother's wife, in case I never mentioned it) applied a lot of pressure to Dad. When he pushed me away,

I got the feeling it wasn't his idea. He was just trying to sort of keep the peace.
So, now I'm in danger of going down another rabbit hole.
Do I try to figure ALL of this out, or just take it one step at a time and see what happens?
Stupid question. I already know the answer. One step at a time.
I'll try not to overthink the rest of it.
It's so much. It's almost too much.
How do I do this? How do I reconnect? What does that take?
And, even if I do, it wouldn't, it can't, bring Troy back, can it?
I need to talk to you about it. I need to hear what you think.
I need a beer.
I'm actually drinking coffee. Again. The pot was cleaner than it has been in years.
Thank you for that. The coffee tastes great.

Jack put the notebook down, set his feet on the coffee table, and held the warm cup with both hands. The gas fireplace was still lit, adding its warmth to the room, and he felt his shoulders relax and drop an inch or two. Given the mimosas, the cozy fire, and the sex, Jack had a fleeting moment of bliss, of perfect contentment—until reality intruded and thoughts of his father's message brought his shoulders back to attention.

River Van Beek caught the big one, or so he believed, and had he been holding a fishing pole, the tip would have bent decisively toward the water. When he saw the woman walking dejectedly toward him from Jack's door, he was sure it was the female half of the couple he'd spent his day tracking. Who else could it be?

After taking her photo, River grabbed his canvas satchel and made his way to the door. He paused just inside, waiting to see which way she would turn down Main Street, hoping to follow her undetected. When she didn't make a turn at the corner, but headed across the street straight toward him, River had a moment of panic. Had he been exposed? Had someone from Coffee Emporium alerted them to his questions? Described him? River very nearly peed his pants, at least a little.

When the woman stopped short of the coffee shop and instead opened the door of the blue BMW parked directly in front of it, River breathed a sigh of relief. As she began to pull away, he exited the cafe, as quickly and inconspicuously as his brown suit would allow, and jumped in his own car, which was parked right behind her. He tossed the canvas satchel onto the passenger seat, started the car, and pulled away from the curb, falling in behind the Beemer. While she waited to turn at the first light, he jotted down her license plate.

River couldn't remember a time he'd felt so exhilarated. Certainly not since he tried scuba diving four years earlier. Much like his attempt to discreetly follow the woman he believed to be Aria, he found scuba diving both exciting and terrifying, especially the time he was forced to surface faster than he expected. He couldn't control his breathing and used up his air tank at twice the rate of his fellow divers. But, unlike diving, tailing the blue Beemer required little to no athleticism, only cunning and patience, two qualities River believed he carried in abundance.

The driver of the BMW moved cautiously down the snow-covered street so, to make sure he wasn't spotted, River stayed at least three car lengths behind her at all times. Other than having watched uncountable hours of old cop shows, River had no training, formal or informal, in tailing another vehicle, so he couldn't be sure if three car lengths was exactly the right distance. She didn't seem to notice him at all, which, for River, was not unusual when it came to women, but this time he was happy about it.

The BMW wound its way to the I-75 on-ramp with River, in his old Ford Focus—its varicolored panels not at all inconspicuous—following suit. Most of the snow had already been cleared from the highway and traffic was moving at normal speed as River quietly chased "Aria" north toward the suburbs.

But where are we going? Didn't the coffee people tell me she lived in an apartment not far from the shop? Why was she parked there when she could have easily walked?

River began to doubt what he was doing.

Or was it the guy who lived up the street?

Now River was doubting the details of the conversations he'd had with the coffee shop workers. He'd begun to believe he was following the wrong person.

Aria awoke after a short nap. She had to pee. Jack was no longer in bed; he'd managed to slip away without waking her. Though naked, she was warm, even lacking Jack's body heat, but still slipped on "her" sweats as she got out of bed. On her way up the stairs, she decided that even though wearing Jack's clothes made her feel closer to him, it was time to change into something that actually fit her, even if it wasn't as comfortable as the sweats. She was pretty sure Jack had put their clothes in the dryer, she just wasn't sure if she wanted to wear her river clothes until they had been washed two or three more times.

She found Jack on the couch, enjoying the fire and another cup of coffee.

Aria came up behind him and wrapped her arms around his shoulders. She whispered in his ear. "Mmm . . . you feel good. You doing okay up here?"

Jack turned to kiss her, being careful not to spill the hot coffee.

"I'm okay, I think. Yeah. I'm feeling okay. Just trying to decide what my next move should be."

Aria's first reaction was to say, "Call your father, dummy," but she managed to suppress it and stay focused on her immediate mission. "Feel like a field trip?"

"Absolutely. Where to?"

"I figured it was time to change out of your sweats, as much as I love them. I need to get into my closet and find something a little more form-fitting. Can you help me pick something?"

"I'm in. But you know I washed your clothes. They should be dry by now."

"Yeah, I know, but I'm thinking those might just end up in the trash. Help me pick some clothes that haven't been infused with river germs."

Jack wasn't sure how much help he could provide to Aria but was happy to join the quest. His fashion sense was not well-developed and he'd learned early in life not to offer an opinion when asked by a woman about the appeal of one outfit or another, even if they appeared to want the truth. But Jack understood there was more at play than Aria's desire to rope him into helping her pick an outfit. He guessed correctly that she was afraid to leave him alone, that she worried he was again standing on the precipice of a pit of despair and, as a result, needed watching. No matter Aria's reasons for keeping Jack close by, he had no desire to be otherwise. He was ready to follow her around all day if the situation called for it. And all night. And all the next day.

"Do you mind if I change before we go? If you're going to put on something presentable I should probably lose the clown pants." He took her hand and led her toward his room and wardrobe.

Aria giggled. "Fair enough. But I'll miss them, and I think you will too."

"I promise I'll wear them whenever you want."

It felt good to promise her something, felt good to promise her something that would happen in the *future*, not just something that would happen today. In fact, it felt so good to make the future promise he wanted to make more of them, and not just ones about clown pants. Aria was unaware of what was going on in Jack's head, but had she known she would have understood that any fears she had about leaving Jack unattended were unfounded. He had no plans to go anywhere without her.

Jack started changing, happy to be doing more than drinking spiked coffee and dozing on the couch. He'd removed his shirt and was about to strip off the clown pants when he remembered he was "going commando." For reasons he didn't fully understand, he suddenly felt shy about standing naked in front of Aria. It made no sense, really, given what they'd done with and to each other over the last eight hours or so. But Jack turned away from Aria, pulled off the clown pants and replaced them with a pair of clean boxer briefs as quickly as possible. It occurred to him he could have just gone into the bathroom, but felt that would have been too obvious, too weird.

Aria watched the scene unfold, amused and somewhat bewildered by his embarrassment. She didn't speak until she was sure he'd finished dressing.

"You ready to go?"

"Umm. Give me a minute." Jack tilted his head toward the bathroom. "Coffee's catching up with me."

"Good point! I'll use the other," Aria said as she jogged up the stairs.

Bladders now empty, they donned coats and began the trudge to Aria's place through mostly un-shoveled snow. For her, the trip was much more comfortable than the one she'd made earlier. This time she had her coat, returned by Tracy, which was warm and dry and an excellent defense against the cold.

The trip was short and soon Aria was buzzing them through the resident's door. She guided Jack up the steps to her apartment and, keys at the ready, opened the door. She couldn't remember a time she was happier to walk through it into her apartment. The interior was warm and familiar. This was *her* place.

Jack was somewhat less thrilled than Aria. The first thing he noticed was the mess. It couldn't be missed. And it wasn't just the mess, it was the breadth of the mess. It caught him completely by surprise. At his place, she'd done such a great job cleaning the coffee carafe that Jack naturally extrapolated Aria's cleaning habits were universal, applying to all places at all times. After all, at work she kept the bar spotlessly clean, so Jack was taken aback by the state of her residence. And what a state it was. Jack quietly compared it to a war zone as Aria beckoned him with a wave of her hand.

Is she a hoarder?

Jack suddenly realized how little he really knew about her.

Aria laughed nervously. "Sorry about the mess."

Jack smiled uncomfortably as he attempted to maneuver over and around the piles of clothes that hid the floor beneath them. Unsure as to their washed/unwashed condition, he did his best not to step on them as he fell in behind Aria. There were clothes everywhere, not just on the floor. Every flat surface in the great room, including the kitchen island, was covered. Aria's wardrobe was expansive, and strewn about in such a way so as to deny Jack the opportunity to discern the color of the carpet, couch, or chairs.

At least it doesn't smell.

While Jack contemplated what forces must have been at play for this Big Bang-like explosion of clothes to come into being, Aria got busy looking for the right outfit, something suitable for either a winter walk or a parental cocktail party, or both. To Jack, it appeared Aria knew exactly what she was doing, knew exactly what she was looking for and where it was located. To the best of his knowledge, she'd not created a map, nothing involving numbered quadrants where certain categories of clothing were located. If such a map existed, it was only in her head. This fact piqued his curiosity, and revved up his engineer's brain. He watched Aria's meticulous movements with a sort of wonder, like watching a ten-year-old defeat an aging chess master in the park.

"Oh . . . sorry about the mess. I wasn't expecting company." Aria, embarrassed, apologized again. She'd had no one in her apartment since her roommate moved out six months before and, over that time, had co-opted the spare bedroom and the living room as extra closet space. Aria didn't consider the havoc to be a problem, exactly. "You know, I've got a lot of clothes. I haven't really changed, well, grown, I mean, since I was fifteen."

"No, no." Jack protested. "I'm just impressed with how you seem to know where everything is hiding. I suppose, though, that it would be nice for you to have a place to sit."

Aria felt her face flush. "Yeah, I'm sorry about this. I should get rid of most of this. Goodwill or something. Do you think I'm a hoarder?"

Jack trod carefully. "Do *you* think you're a hoarder?"

Aria giggled nervously. "Maybe a little? I don't like to throw things out, and that, you know, sort of got worse after Steffi died." She waved her arm over the expanse. "Plus, like I said, everything still fits. You know what I mean?"

"Well, you know, if you ever want any help getting the stuff you don't want to Goodwill, I'm your man. Whenever you're ready. In the meantime, I'll just uncover a chair and wait while you find what you're looking for."

Aria still felt self-conscious, and wondered how she allowed this to happen. She hurried to find the right clothes, not just because she wanted to be warm and comfortable, but also because she wanted to get Jack out of her apartment as soon as possible. She would clean all this up before Monday, she decided. And if the thrift store wasn't open, she'd just give everything away on the street. Or throw it in a dumpster. *No, that would be wasteful. Goodwill it is.* And she had no intention of inviting Jack to assist. He'd already suffered enough.

Aria found the clothes for which she'd been searching and went into her bedroom to change. She didn't escape to the bedroom because she was uncomfortable changing in front of Jack, but seeing Jack sitting amongst the piles had made her sheepish about anything involving her clothes.

Aria emerged from the bedroom after taking time to pull her hair into a ponytail and put on some makeup. She did these things for herself, to feel presentable, but the effects of these efforts were not lost on Jack. The transformation caught him by surprise and drew his focus from the textile debris field with which he was surrounded.

Beautiful.

Aria was only slightly aware of Jack's admiring stare. "Are you hungry? Do you want to get some lunch? I think we're both finally dressed for it."

The question broke Jack from his little Aria trance. "Yes. Absolutely."

They left her apartment and ventured up the street to a shawarma place, surprised and pleased that it was open despite the storm and the intermittent, falling snow. Though open, the weather had denied the restaurant an abundance of customers, or barely any customers at all, and Jack and Aria were greeted by an employee whose less-than-emotive demeanor made it impossible to determine if she was pleased or annoyed by their presence. There were only two other customers visible in the dining area.

"Table for two?"

Aria answered before Jack had the chance. "We'll just sit at the bar."

This seemed to please the greeter, who smiled ever so slightly as her new patrons climbed onto two of the bar stools while she set menus in front of them.

"Lisa will be helping you." The hostess did not inform Jack and Aria as to Lisa's whereabouts or when to expect her arrival, so they took their time examining the menu.

Jack started flipping through the pages. "Do you think they were getting ready to close up?"

"No idea. Maybe, if it keeps snowing. We might have lucked out."

Indeed, the shawarma place was the first open restaurant they'd found on their walk down Main Street and despite the ambivalence of the hostess, Lisa appeared a mercifully short time later, before either had managed to choose their respective meals.

"Can I get you guys a drink?"

Jack and Aria looked at each other, each waiting for the other to cue them on whether they were going to keep the alcohol flowing.

Jack spoke up first. "Can I say something blasphemous?"

"Of course. I expect nothing less."

"I could really use some water."

Aria laughed and looked at Lisa. "Two waters, please. And we'll need a minute or two with the menu."

Relieved, Aria did not take issue with a break from drinking, even if she *was* craving a glass of wine, and Jack appreciated her willingness to take charge. He was not surprised by it, just pleased, figuring her experience behind the bar at Liberty's lent itself to the easygoing manner with which she was handling herself. Or maybe she'd always been that way. Jack didn't know for sure but was enticed by the prospect of finding out, even if it took years.

Jack and Aria ordered and received their food in no time. They ate the hummus and chicken shawarma in near silence, not allowing conversation to interfere with the sating of their ravenous appetites. From their perches at the bar, they observed a few more customers wander in and receive the same cool reception from the hostess, but mostly concentrated on the task at hand—making food disappear.

Stomachs full and warm, they confidently reentered the world outside of the restaurant. The snow had stopped but the sky was still cloudy and they were as comfortable as they'd been in hours and hours. Aria especially felt back to normal, no longer having to wear Jack's workout gear. She did, however, look forward to the opportunity to wear his clothes again, only on a more voluntary basis. Though she felt far more herself in her own clothes, they didn't protect her from the whipping wind nearly as well as Jack's thick sweatshirt and sweatpants.

River was finally convinced he was following the wrong person, which was disappointing. Now he needed to come up with a new plan.

Start from the beginning.

This was what his editor had told him time and time again, and River had taken the advice to heart. Having tailed the wrong person for nearly twenty minutes, he turned his car around and headed back to the coffee shop, back to where he'd seen the woman emerge from the apartment behind Liberty's. After all, he told himself, her appearance had been the only "success" he'd experienced since stumbling across the story in the first place. River was confident he would get to the bottom of things. All he had to do was start over.

River made it back to Main Street in surprisingly short order and was again struck by the emptiness of the sidewalks. Due to the storm, the street was nearly devoid of foot traffic, as it had been before he left on the wild goose chase. People were hunkered down in their apartments, he figured, getting cozy under blankets and drinking hot chocolate, all while he was out trying to track down a story.

River saw them as he drove slowly up the one-way street, back to the coffee shop. He saw the couple carefully navigating the snow-covered sidewalk, hand in hand. They were hard to miss, considering they were the only people to *be* seen. He got a pretty good look at them when he was forced to stop at a light. They were talking to each other, smiling, enjoying each other despite the cold and the snow. It made River sad.

John Current started pacing around the kitchen island. It had been hours since he'd left a message for his son, hours since he decided he had to hear his son's voice. Susan had come and gone a couple of times already, but the expected argument never materialized. Maybe she was starting to feel like he did. Maybe she was as exhausted as he. He hoped that was true.

Chapter Eleven

A River Runs Through It

It took River a minute to figure out why the happy couple made him sad. Though he could've used that minute to put two and two together, to create a theory about how these two people might be the same ones for whom he'd been searching, he instead used the time to pine, to remember that he'd never really had a serious relationship with a woman. He didn't know if it was his weight, or the expanding bald spot, or perhaps the fact he wasn't very funny or charming. And it wasn't that he didn't want to have a girlfriend, a "significant other." He did. Definitely. He just didn't know how to go about it.

These were the things chewing up River's attention span as he parked his car and returned to the chair in the coffee shop, across the street from the orange building. Across the street from Liberty's. The chair had grown cold in his absence, but he would sit long enough, staring across the street, for his ass to warm it in short order. River would kick himself for it later, but while he was obsessing over his lack of prowess with the opposite sex, the people for whom he'd been looking returned to the apartment he'd spent hours stalking.

Jack and Aria did not intend to sneak into his apartment and were, in fact, unaware they were sneaking at all. After all, they didn't know the Mad Knocker was just across the street, waiting for them from his perch in the coffee shop. Nor did they know his name was River, or that he was a reporter for the local newspaper. Of all this they were blissfully unaware as they made their way back from lunch. Jack did notice the car, however, the one waiting at a stop sign. He noticed the car because it was, at the moment, the only one on the street. For sure there would be more cars later, after the snow melted a little, but for now there was just the one. Jack didn't bother to try to see who was driving it; he was too involved with Aria to care.

"Do you want to consider that our second date?" Aria teased Jack as he opened the door for her, poking him playfully in the stomach as she moved through the doorway. At this, Jack grabbed her wrist, held her in place, pulled her close and kissed her mouth before releasing her seconds later with a smile.

They'd returned from the restaurant feeling strangely upbeat, holding hands the entire walk. This hopefulness may have been the result of a good lunch, or the fact that nothing unusual had happened in the last thirty-three minutes. Regardless, the touching enhanced their mood, or was at least an expression of it.

Aria felt especially buoyant, though she was unsure exactly why. But it didn't matter. It didn't matter that the last twenty hours had been a whirlwind. It didn't matter that she'd survived falling into a cold, slow-moving body of water. What mattered to her, in that moment, and in all the moments in the foreseeable future, was that she'd fallen in love. She'd fallen in love with a man at least as flawed as she, likely more so. Well, clearly more so. It didn't matter why. That was for another day. And maybe the "why" didn't even matter. She was happy. And she wanted Jack to be happy too.

When Jack pulled her close, when he wouldn't immediately let her through the open door, his eyes locked with hers and she felt a thrill, a rush. She realized, as Jack helped her with her coat, that it had been a long, long time since she'd felt that charge, that chemistry. The kiss was amazing.

What to do?

Free Will

Aria knew she could allow herself to be carried away. She could let the stream running between them take her away, take her toward love's blissful oblivion. She could picture them on the couch, in front of the fire, maybe reading. She could see them cooking together, making more cocktails, maybe binge-watching Dr. Who. They would share the same bed every night, and coffee (with Kahlua) every morning. She could see them never leaving Jack's apartment. They would be happy. They would ask the world to leave them alone. And it might actually comply, at least for a little while. At least for a snow day. Maybe two.

But not right now, she told herself. Don't get lost. Not yet. There was unfinished business.

"Jack."

Aria wasn't sure why, exactly, his name chose to escape her mouth at that moment. But her thoughts had gotten ahead of her, and everything was roiling and something was bound to come out and it just happened to be Jack's name and now she felt like an idiot. Aria raced to say something more, something she'd already been thinking.

"I think you should call your father."

The pronouncement startled Jack. He'd managed, during the trip to Aria's and lunch at the shawarma place, to push the message from his father into a recess in the back of his brain, into a drawer of his mind's filing cabinet he'd not opened in almost a year. Before Aria spoke up, Jack's thoughts had safely wandered to nothing deeper than the volume of the remaining Kahlua, the bottle thus far bottomless.

"Do you think the coffee is still good?"

It was Aria's turn to be startled. Jack's non-answer to her question was unexpected. She paused before she answered.

"Yes, I do. I'm sure it's fine. But . . . did you hear the part about calling your father?"

Yes, of course I heard that part.

"Yes. I did. I'm just not sure I'm ready. It's been almost a year, Aria. I mean, what am I supposed to say to him?"

"Okay, yeah, good question." Aria thought for a moment, the idea of a quiet day in front of the fire melting in the face of reality. She did, after all, consider the current problem temporary. "I don't know the answer. But I think that's just because I don't know everything and, you know, just because I don't know everything doesn't mean you shouldn't call him. You know?"

Jack, now thoroughly confused, wasn't sure what Aria was asking. "Huh?"

Aria took a deep breath. "What I mean is that you should go ahead and call him. You don't need to plan what you're going to say. He sounds like he already knows what he wants to say to you."

Jack considered Aria's words as he poured more Kahlua into his mug. The bottle was still surprisingly heavy, indicating its contents were not disappearing as quickly as he'd feared.

"Want one?" He waved the mug in Aria's direction, pointing at it with the index finger of his other hand.

"Okay, yes please."

Aria didn't think she wanted another Kahlua and coffee until the moment Jack asked her, at which point she loved the idea. A nearly perfect combination of depressant and stimulant, the drink itself was a metaphor for how she thought life itself should work. It would neither make her more tired nor less. It would keep her on a keel she felt had substantially evened out over the last few hours, even considering the small tempest created by the call from Jack's father.

Contemplating the finer things had distracted Aria from the issue at hand. She regrouped and took a sip from the recharged mug.

"Ooh, this is good. Thanks, Jack. But can we talk about your father for a minute?"

Free Will

Jack really didn't want to talk about his father, or mother, or family. A discussion of that type, he felt, would definitely destroy the positive effects of the Kahlua, and he was enjoying those effects. His heart rate had leveled off, and he could feel just a little buzz, manifested, he assumed, either by the Kahlua or the coffee or both. It was probably both. Regardless, he was enjoying the buzz and didn't want it to disappear, at least not until it occurred to him that the buzzing might be alerting him to the possibility of a stroke.

"Do you know the symptoms of a stroke?"

"A what?" Aria was confused.

"A stroke."

"No, I don't. Sorry. Do you think you might be having a stroke?"

Jack thought for a minute. "Well, no. I suppose. Not really. I've just got this pleasant feeling and I thought it was possible it could be a stroke."

Aria decided to go along with Jack's avoidance tactic and, for the moment, abandoned her attempt to corral him into a conversation about his father.

"So, you feel good, but you're not sure why, so it must be a stroke. Did I get that right?"

"Well, you know, when you put it that way you make me sound crazy." Jack took a sip of his drink, keeping his eyes on Aria over the lip of the mug.

Aria laughed and decided to stop trying to corner Jack about his father. She didn't see the point in badgering him and believed doing so served no purpose other than to cause him to retreat further into whatever cave he'd already retreated. Besides, when she took a pause, she realized how annoying she sounded. So she dropped it. For now.

"How much Kahlua is left?"

Jack picked up the bottle to again check its weight, smiling as he set the bottle back down.

"Infinity and beyond, apparently."

"Great. Let's fill up and retire to the couch. That big lunch is making me tired."

Jack topped off their drinks and pondered the myriad things that likely had a hand in making Aria tired. The list included: "Hunting Jack Down in a Snowstorm," "Jumping Off a Bridge and Almost Drowning," and "Spending Hours and Hours in a Hospital Getting Tested for Suicidal Behavior."

Jack completed the list in the time it took to top off their drinks and sit down with Aria. He was happy to sit down as well, thus far having experienced all the same things as Aria, except for the "Hunting Jack Down in a Snowstorm" part. Still, he'd been on his own mission the night before, one that led him down the same streets. He had every excuse to be as tired as she.

Aria's eyes started to close soon after they sat down, though she fought it. She had so much on her mind, so much to say, so much to understand. Intellectually, she understood all would be resolved or revealed over time, that she needed more than a day for everything to make sense. But it was hard to fight the desire to know now. Still, she was losing the battle; the Kahlua had gotten the upper hand over the coffee. She leaned into Jack, surrounded by the scent of whatever soap he used and the heat of the fire.

Jack knew the moment Aria was asleep. She slumped into him, ever so slightly, and her breathing changed. It made him happy she was able to do this, though he understood there were more forces at work than her desire to be near him. At this point, he thought, she might have been able to fall asleep against a telephone pole, or any other surface, so long as it was unmoving.

Free Will

And that was part of the problem. For Jack, the *coffee* had the upper hand, and he sat wide awake next to Aria, wondering how to amuse himself without waking his brand-new girlfriend. He could read, he thought, if he could get to a book. He'd rejected reading earlier that day but now was feeling more amenable to the idea—any distraction would do at this point. But the books were too far away, and he'd not figured out how to create a convincing "Jack" substitute against which Aria could lean. There was an abundance of within-reach couch pillows but getting them in place before Aria fell over was a potential pitfall, so he rejected the idea, at least momentarily. It was more important for her to sleep than for him to read.

The notebook, however, taunted him from less than two feet away. It called to him from the coffee table, daring him to write something, anything. Jack carefully considered the dilemma, and convinced himself he could overcome the problem. All he needed to do, he postulated, was to gently move Aria to a prone position, maybe even manage to get a pillow under her head.

The attempt started slowly, with Jack inching away from the couch back and turning toward Aria's slumping corpse. It didn't take long for him to get the hang of it, and he managed to extricate himself without waking her. He gently lifted her head and slid a pillow underneath.

Success!

1:20 PM
Jeez! How many times are you going to fall asleep on the couch today?
Just kidding, of course. I know how comfortable that couch can be.
And you're invited to sleep on it whenever you want.
Listen, I realize you're very interested in me calling Dad.

I know you want me to reconnect with my family.
Trust me, I want that, too. But it's been so long. It will take a minute. More than a minute.
I'm working through it, even as I'm writing. Right now.
Don't worry, though. I'll get there. I'm getting there.
And I swear you'll be the first to know when I am.
On a different, random topic – what do you think about all these books?
I'm sitting here staring at them.
They're not all mine. They were here when I moved in. Did I tell you this already?
I think they make me look well-read, or maybe snooty.
I've never heard of half of them. I mean, who the hell is Alfred Lord Tennyson?
What a funny name.
So far no one has asked about the books, but that may be because I don't have people over.
Not for a while, anyway.
The fewer visitors, the fewer questions.
I think I've had more people in the house today than I've had in a year, especially if you count the knocking guy, even though we didn't let him in.
Jeez. Not even sure why I'm talking about this. I suppose I could use some sleep too.

River's butt was getting sore. He hadn't seen anyone on the street since his return to the coffee shop. The crowd had dwindled, the shop occupied now only by River, the barista, and an old guy steadily typing on his computer, a wooden cane resting next to him on the banquette. River wondered sarcastically how long the old man had been working on the Great American Novel, then decided such a thing probably didn't exist. The last book River tried to read was *Fifty Shades of Grey*, mostly because he wanted to know what all the fuss was about but, for various reasons, only made it to page 80 before giving up. What he mostly remembered about the book was how many times he read the word "murmur."

River pulled his attention away from the old man's typing and returned it to the window to look out over Main Street at the orange building. The sky was still gray but had lightened a little. The snow had stopped and some of it was melting with the rising temperature.

River was at a loss. He'd wasted a goodly amount of time chasing the wrong car and putting miles on his own, which was not an easy decision. He knew his old Focus wasn't long for this world, that the scrapyard was calling, at least that's what his mechanic told him, as did the mechanic from whom he sought a second opinion. It turned out the car just didn't have the wherewithal to drive much over 220,000 miles.

But River's car wasn't really the issue. He could always borrow his mother's when his finally broke down. His internal debate instead centered on whether or not he should continue what he was doing; if it was worth it to sit in the coffee shop and stare at the door of a building that may not have anyone behind it. After all, he hadn't seen anyone leave or enter since chasing after the wrong car. Doubt began to overwhelm him. River Van Beek needed guidance and encouragement.

He called his editor.

"River? Why are you calling me on a Saturday? Everything okay?"

Perry "Bob" White honestly liked River. Though most of the newsroom denizens continued to treat River like an intern, Perry believed in River's potential, and had said as much to him and the powers-that-be. Sure, River could be needy, like now, but Perry truly believed he would become a good reporter. Someday. Sometime in the future.

"Well, Bob, I'm not sure." Perry insisted on being called Bob, eschewing his given name so as not to be confused with Clark Kent's editor at the Daily Planet.

"Tell me what's going on, River."

River dove into the narrative of his morning, all the events that had transpired since he first came across the story of the possibility that alligators, or perhaps lungfish, had crawled out of the river, and ending with him sitting in the nearly empty coffee shop talking with his boss on a Saturday afternoon. River made sure to omit no detail, wanting to prove to his editor that he had a grasp of the facts.

"What's your next move, River?"

River paused, confused. "Well, I guess I don't really know. I was hoping you would."

"Hmm. Do you have the story yet?"

"Well, no, I guess. I'm just sitting here waiting for something to happen."

"Listen, River. We've talked about this before. The waiting is one of the worst parts of the job, but it's something we all have to do. News doesn't happen in the newsroom. You know that."

River did know that. "News Doesn't Happen in the Newsroom" was one of Bob's favorite quotes. He never let his reporters forget it. The quote was on a banner hanging on the wall behind Bob's desk.

"You're right, Bob. I'll keep waiting."

"Do you have anything better to do?"

River thought for a minute, but the extra time he used to think about the question wasn't really necessary. "No."

"Have at it then. If it's any consolation, the paper will pick up the cost of your coffee. Just make sure you get a receipt."

River didn't find the joke particularly funny.

Free Will

Jack's father was finished with the newspaper. He'd been finished with the newspaper for at least an hour, having read every article that held any interest for him, and some that held none. Still, he sat, reflexively checking his phone even as he tried to distract himself from it. Had it rung and he missed it? John checked and the phone confirmed he'd missed nothing. He turned the ringer volume up as high as it would go, just to be sure.

Chapter Twelve

He Won't Get Far on Foot

Aria woke to quiet warmth. Unsure of how long she'd been asleep, she assumed it had been hours. Her phone told her it had been only minutes.

Power nap.

She couldn't decide if she wanted to get up from the couch, or even sit up, fearing anything that altered her comfortably prone position would alter everything. And that was the last thing she desired. Altering. Believing she'd found the coziest position she'd ever experienced; she didn't want to move. But even as Aria reveled in record-setting repose, she wondered about Jack's whereabouts. The wondering was not demanding enough to make her sit up, so she remained motionless, head resting on a couch pillow, facing the bookshelves.

Aria gazed about the room to the extent possible. Her position did not allow for a wide-ranging field of vision but was sufficient for her to recognize that Jack was in neither of the chairs across from her, nor sitting in front of the fire. Switching senses, Aria focused on sound. She could hear the hiss of gas from the fireplace, the footsteps of Jack's upstairs neighbor, and warm air being forced into the room through the floor vents. But she caught no audible sign of Jack's presence.

Maybe he's downstairs?

The idea was problematic, if that was the case. Verifying Jack's location in the bedroom necessarily meant she would have to vacate the couch, something she was loathe to do, given her current level of comfort. At that moment, a ray of sunlight pierced the low cover of gray and, reflecting off an upper-story pane across the street, penetrated the north-facing window to fall upon Aria's face. The ray of light was not only a pleasant revision of the day's dominant weather pattern, but its arrival coincided with the advent of Aria's simple and elegant idea for locating Jack without having to undertake any major, physical movement.

I can just call him.

Aria told herself she was a genius. She only had to use her arm and hand to implement her revelatory idea. Jack answered on the third ring.

"Hey! I didn't think you'd be awake yet." Jack's breathing indicated he was in motion.

"Me neither, but I'm doing a pretty good job of not moving at all. I'm going to steal your couch, I think. Where are you?"

"I'm out. Decided to take a walk. I just needed some time to think. I hope I didn't wake you."

Aria supposed it was possible the sound of the door opening and closing woke her from slumber, but wasn't about to say that to Jack.

"You didn't. No way. I think the silence woke me up. Or maybe it was your neighbor stomping around upstairs."

Jack laughed. "That's Tom. He's usually pretty quiet. The difference might be snow boots."

"Do you mind if I just stay on your couch for a while?"

You can stay there forever.

"Please do. I'll be back in a few. Like I said, I'm just clearing my head a little."

"Okay, see you soon."

Aria set her phone down, right next to the notebook. Continuing to employ minimal effort and movement, she grabbed it and opened to the last entry, reading it and managing to remain on her side as she held the page aloft, in front of her face.

Aria knew she should respond right away, to make sure she wrote something to Jack in case she again dozed off and before he got back.

> *1:35 PM*
> *Yeah, your place is like a train station. That's sarcasm, if you were wondering. You know, I can't remember if you told me about the books or not. (We're both tired, I guess.) But I like them. I feel like if you remove the books the shelves might just float away. Nothing to hold them down. Plus, what's the purpose of a bookshelf if not to hold books? I suppose that all the books help the shelf fulfill its purpose. Don't you think? I don't think it matters if you've read them or not. Either way, I like that they're sitting there, looking sophisticated and literary.*
> *And, yes, I definitely want you to reconnect with your family, but I don't want to be pushy. You'll be ready when you're ready. It's up to you, of course. You're allowed to take things at your own pace, in your own time. You don't have to do what anyone tells you, not even me, even though I'm wise beyond my years.*
> *By the way, did I mention this is the most wonderful couch in the world? I think the couch, the Kahlua, and the heat from the fire create a perfect storm for sleeping. That sounds weird doesn't it, a perfect storm for sleeping? I mean, storms are usually loud and scary. Not this one. This one puts me to sleep. And keeps me from drooling, apparently.*
> *But why aren't you asleep? Why is all this working for me but not you? Maybe we're reacting differently to our little drug cocktails. Or maybe you've just got too much on your mind. Either way, you don't know what you're missing.*
> *See you soon.*

Jack hung up, put the phone in his pants pocket, and kept walking. He was sure his exit had awakened Aria, despite her assertion to the contrary. But he really did need to clear his head; he needed a few minutes to let the call from his father sink in.

As he walked, rounding corners and crossing streets, Jack took note of the numerous bars, in particular the ones where he'd spent time the night before. They seemed different now, and not just because they were closed or because the light was different. The difference was in him.

This thought hadn't yet occurred to Jack, but was creeping up on him, especially as he considered his new reality, his new circumstance. One change he did notice, by the time he'd put a couple of blocks between himself and his apartment, was his posture. The night before, as he wandered from bar to bar, he'd kept his head down, mostly staring at the pavement in front of his feet and the blank, white canvas stretched before him.

Now his head was up, his back straight. And although he still felt the dull ache in his hip about every third step, today, for the first time in a year, it was not accompanied by an acute emotional pain that weighed on him more than the injury. Jack walked as if he owned the buildings around him, and the snow did not bother him or slow him down. He couldn't remember ever feeling so light.

And, of course, there was Aria.

Where had she come from, he wondered. To what prayer was she the answer?

All of them.

Buried in thought, Jack didn't notice the short, chubby man in a large, crumpled overcoat following a block behind him; River was doing his best not to be seen. He felt lucky to have spotted the man, who he believed to be Jack Current, emerge from the door across the street, and waited until Jack was a safe distance down the sidewalk before he left the coffee shop. With the barista's permission, River left his satchel and ventured back out into the snow, taking only his notebook.

River was exhilarated. He felt sure that this time he was tailing the right person; that he wasn't wasting his time. River also figured Jack wouldn't get far on foot and he should be able to keep up, especially considering the snow. Jack certainly wasn't going to walk to the suburbs, not with that limp, however slight.

Wait. Where did that limp come from? The car accident? The river?

River hadn't noticed it until then. Of course, he wasn't sure exactly who he was following. He simply hoped it was Jack Current. Now, however, his confidence level was high. Maybe Jack would stop somewhere. River hoped he would. If he did stop somewhere, the opportunity to ask questions might present itself. He could get some answers. Maybe.

Even though he was absolutely positive he wouldn't end up in the 'burbs, it turned out River did have a problem keeping up with Jack, despite Jack's bum leg. After a block or two, River started to fall behind and had to force himself to speed up to keep an acceptable distance behind Jack, far enough behind not to be noticed but still close enough not to lose him.

River's lungs started to burn, just a little. He hadn't walked that far or that fast in some time, maybe never, and he cursed himself for giving up his gym membership, the one he never used. The snow was still melting, but slowly. There was plenty on the sidewalks to impede his steps, and he cursed Jack for going so fast, and cursed himself for not being able to keep up. Then, for good measure, he cursed the snow.

The reporter had no idea where Jack might be headed. It seemed he was walking in circles, or squares, considering the geometry of city blocks. What River noticed, when his attention wasn't consumed with maintaining just the right distance from Jack, was how many bars and restaurants were located along their route. River had never spent much time in Over-the-Rhine and was surprised by how many buildings had been renovated, the street level housing some retail, but mostly eating and drinking establishments. There was no lack of them.

River decided he would visit them, at least a few of them, sometime when he wasn't "on the job." This thought reminded him that he was hungry, and he paused a moment to look at the menu posted in a restaurant window. He glanced back at Jack just in time to see him make an unexpected right turn. His quarry disappeared quickly, forcing River to forget his stomach and resume the pursuit at an even quicker pace.

Jack did not have a route mapped out; instead he just walked around, letting his brain work through the problem. Though he didn't have a destination, he didn't leave the neighborhood. He was just out to clear his head, not to make long-lasting, permanent life choices, the kind that required longer walks. Besides, Aria was still on the couch in his living room, so he didn't want to wander too far. She might need him, though he doubted it. Thus far she had proven resilient and self-sufficient, something he appreciated.

Nearly everything was closed and Jack figured it was the snow, but by then it had stopped falling and the streets and sidewalks were slowly clearing. It was afternoon, and he wasn't used to the neighborhood being so quiet, especially on a Saturday. He saw few people, and those mostly had snow shovels in their hands. Even the panhandlers, generally omnipresent, were absent.

There *was* someone walking behind him, though. Jack had noticed a man in an overcoat at least a block or so back but couldn't make out the face. Despite the morning's encounters with the Mad Knocker and the questioner at Coffee Emporium, Jack told himself not to be paranoid.

It seemed, however, that the stranger was attempting to match his pace, slowing down and speeding up when necessary. This inflamed Jack's paranoia, and he began to theorize that maybe this person was, indeed, following him. So, after catching the besuited stalker a couple more times out of the corner of his eye, Jack decided to test his theory. The test was simple, and one he'd seen in any number of cops-and-robbers movies as a child.

Jack made an abrupt turn at the next corner and, once out of sight, ran to the first alley and crouched down behind a snow-covered dumpster. Less than a minute passed before the dumpy man in the wrinkled trench coat lumbered by. The man failed to notice Jack's lurking, but Jack was able to get a good look at him as he wandered past the dumpster.

Jack's quick thinking yielded results. He was able to confirm that he had, indeed, been followed and yes, by the same man they'd seen in Coffee Emporium that morning, the one asking questions about him and Aria. Though he had no idea who the man could be, Jack guessed correctly that the short fellow was the Mad Knocker, and that he was either a cop or a reporter.

Jack gave the man enough time to put a little distance between them before emerging from his hiding place and, on impulse, started following *him*.

The hunter becomes the hunted.

River wasn't sure what could have happened to the man he was following. He didn't think he'd fallen too far behind him, though he knew it was possible. In any case, Jack appeared to have vanished. There was no one in sight after he turned the corner and, given his rather limited tracking abilities, he failed to notice the footprints in the snow leading into the alley.

River paused for a moment, wondering what he should do next. The answer was plain, he believed, so he started back toward the coffee shop, his new home away from home. He believed his only other choice was to give up, and he wasn't ready to give up. Not yet anyway. He'd already invested too much in this potential story and wanted to make Perry "Bob" White proud, so he started moving again, hoping his feet would warm quickly once he was back inside.

Now focused on getting back to his perch in the coffee shop, River did not notice Jack fall in behind him, not that he bothered to look. It hadn't occurred to him that Jack might be sneaky, especially since River was confident there was no way Jack could have known he was being followed. He was sure he'd maintained the proper distance, even when he got winded. No, he was sure Jack was clueless to the gum-shoeing.

Still, River returned to the coffee shop with an all-too-familiar feeling of disappointment. He'd never believed his reporting job was going to be easy, but he had to admit that filing stories on local galas and balls was a world away from what he was doing at the moment. For one, nearly all galas and balls were held indoors, in temperature-controlled environments. Until now he'd never been forced to trudge around in the snow, chasing down a story about someone from whom he was trying to hide.

Second, at social events, nearly everyone was willing to talk to the press, especially the event organizers, whose job it was to "put the word out" as much as possible. River was generally required to show up with little more than a notebook and a photographer. The participants, especially after a few drinks, tended to be verbose and forthcoming about how happy they were to be eating, drinking, and dancing for charity.

This was real work, he told himself as he stood at the counter to buy yet another cup of coffee. And the coffee was damn well going on his expense report.

"Hi, Leslie. I'll have another small, dark roast, please."

"No problem, River."

"Could I get one of those blueberry muffins, too?"

"You bet."

The two had been on a first name basis since River returned from the abortive trip to the suburbs. As had been true earlier, there was no line at the counter. It was just River and Leslie.

River paid for the muffin and small coffee, added some cream and sugar, and carried the purchases back to his table in the window, wadding up his trench coat and placing it on the other chair. He didn't know when Leslie's shift ended, but hoped it wouldn't be until after he finished getting his story. The sudden realization of the open-endedness of his own "shift" gave River a moment of fleeting despair, and he was no longer sure he had the wherewithal to spend much more time working on this particular story, the reward for his work thus far non-existent. River attempted to gird himself for what could be a long haul.

News doesn't happen in the newsroom.

He sipped his coffee and stared out the window, noting a stream of people was beginning to materialize on the sidewalk, on the other side of the glass. What River had missed, however, was the man he'd been following ducking into the door of the apartment, the one on which he'd furiously knocked that morning.

Jack watched the man in the trench coat cross Main Street and walk into the coffee shop across from Liberty's. Jack quickly turned the corner, circled around behind the building and ducked into his own apartment, wondering if the Mad Knocker had spotted him. Once inside,

Free Will

Jack convinced himself he'd been missed, or else the man would likely already be knocking on his door again.

Jack hung up his coat and walked into the kitchen. Aria's body was invisible behind the couch back, so Jack assumed she was still asleep. He wasn't quite sure what to do. His telephone was lying on the kitchen island, taunting him, but taunting him as well was the Kahlua bottle, which he'd failed to put away after its most recent use.

What to do? What to do?

Jack grabbed the phone and called his father.

John Current had managed to pull himself away from his phone for a moment, and was standing in front of the open refrigerator, staring at the full shelves. He was feeling hungry, or at least was feeling something that resembled hunger, so he was staring at the shelves, trying to decide if he wanted to eat and, if so, what. The problem was that whatever was on the shelves before him was not registering with John in any way. Nothing spoke to him; nothing jumped out. His mind was elsewhere. At least until the phone rang.

Chapter Thirteen

Only a Phone Call Away

The phone rang once, and then again, tentatively, or so it seemed. Jack didn't know how long he would have to wait before his father picked up the phone, or if he would pick it up at all. John Current may have had second thoughts by then, or may have been influenced and consequently redirected by his mother, Susan. Jack decided to let the phone ring until it flipped to voicemail. The commitment prevented a preemptive hang up.

His father answered on the third ring.

"Jack?"

Pause. Think about what you're saying.

"Yeah, Dad. It's me. I'm . . . returning your call from this morning. Is everything okay?"

The question was bigger than John expected. *Was everything okay?* Of course, it wasn't ok. He hadn't spoken to his son in nearly a year. And why, he wondered, why hadn't he spoken to his son in a year? He knew the answer. Cowardice.

"No, Jack, everything is not okay." John Current was struggling. When he'd called Jack earlier in the day, he had a vision of how he thought the conversation would go, how it would be the beginning of the repair that was needed to bring the family back together. Now, he was struggling. The vision he'd created was crumbling in the face of actually hearing his son's voice. He fought to recollect the words from the script he'd written in his head while he paced around his kitchen earlier that morning.

Jack was confused as well, unsure how to broach a conversation with his father after so long; after killing John's only grandson. Without thinking, Jack sat down in one of the chairs at *his* kitchen island, knees strangely weak. It was difficult to talk, difficult to push the air out of his lungs and over his vocal cords. In his head, he played his father's message before he spoke again.

"I was surprised by the message, Dad. I'm not quite sure what to do with it."

Finally, John thought, a window opened, and he climbed through it as fast as he could. "Honestly, son, neither am I. At least not right at this moment. I was hoping to be cool and collected but, honestly, I experienced a complete brain fog as soon as I heard your voice."

John's voice sounded more natural to him than he'd anticipated; not angry, but tentative, perhaps even hopeful. He smiled to himself.

And Jack was smiling too, almost laughing. Had the moment been somewhat less weighty he would have released the laugh pushing its way up from his stomach. But was it a laugh of joy or relief, or both? It didn't matter. As it was, he made just enough effort to suppress the shake, to enjoy the moment without interrupting or redirecting it.

"We're on the same page, Dad, not sure what to say."

"That's okay, Jack. I know I took you by surprise, but it shouldn't have been a surprise. I'm ashamed for letting this go on as long as it has." John paused to fight back the tears, to shove the frog back down his throat. "And it stops today. Right now. I want to see you, Jack. I want all of us to see you. I want you to come to the house for dinner tonight."

Like his father, Jack found speaking difficult and realized he was nodding "yes" before remembering his father couldn't see his head bobbing up and down. At the end of what seemed like ten minutes of silence, his tightened throat allowed four words to emerge from the cyclone spinning within.

"I'm so sorry, Dad."

He'd said the words before. Many times. But the wall of pain, hurt, and anger had been too thick for the words to penetrate and, as far as he knew, remained so. Jack did not buy into the truth that time heals all wounds. Had he done so, he'd never have ended up on the bridge the night before. And now he was no longer sure if he was apologizing for killing his nephew or for nearly killing himself, or both. His father, of course, did not know about Jack's plan to jump off the bridge, and never would. That fortuitous miscalculation would remain a secret between Jack and Aria. Forever.

Tears now flowed freely down John's face, and he laughed as the wall he'd spent a year building dismantled itself, brick by brick. He didn't know it would be this easy; that it *could* be this easy. Until that moment, he feared he would never see his youngest son again, that the pain and anguish feeding on itself would forever prevent a reconciliation. He was surprised to discover that all it took was for him to talk to his boy, to be brave enough to talk to his boy.

"You never have to say that again, Jack. I know it." John thought of everyone else hurt by the loss of his grandson. "*We* know it."

Another silence ensued while Jack digested the moment. Had his whole family forgiven him? Or was that just his father's wishful thinking? He wasn't sure which; he didn't care which. He would find out soon enough, at least if he agreed to go. Still, he had to ask . . .

"Does Mom know you're doing this?"

The pregnant pause from the other end of the phone answered Jack's question. Then his father laughed.

"No, not yet, Jack. But don't worry, by the time you get here . . . well, let's just say the food will be on the table."

Free Will

Jack wasn't ready to laugh with his father about his mother's level of animosity. She had always been better than her husband at holding a grudge. But he decided it didn't matter. He decided—no, needed—to believe his father that things would be different.

"What time do you want me to show up?"

"Seven o'clock." The speed with which his father responded meant he already had a plan, even if he was the only one in on it.

"Can I bring a friend?"

As Jack asked the question, Aria leapt off the couch and ran past him on her way to the bathroom, leaving a breeze in her wake. Jack did not need to ask what was going on and, besides, was embroiled in his own, pressured moment.

After a brief pause, John answered.

"Of course, Jack. Of course. I'll see you at seven."

"Thanks, Dad."

The sound of Jack's voice drew Aria from her slumber. She didn't move. She couldn't move, now that she understood Jack was talking to his father. The last thing she wanted was to insert herself into *that* conversation. So, she listened, and while she listened she stared at the notebook on the coffee table in front of her, but decided to leave it alone. No matter how much she wanted to, there was no way for her to write in the notebook without Jack noticing.

Aria felt like an interloper. She knew she should try not to listen, try not to eavesdrop, but there was no way for her to *not* eavesdrop. With her hearing on high alert, the best she could do was to not disturb the conversation. She could only hear one side of it, but that was all she needed to perceive how much was understood but unspoken. And then she had to pee.

Aria fought it quietly, without moving. The coffee and Kahlua worked in tandem to force her off the couch, but she knew she could beat it, knew she could control her body's impulse to evacuate. She'd done it before and in moments far less weighty than this one. So, she told her body to stop it, to relax.

At first, it wasn't too bad. Aria was able to fend off her rebellious bladder and still devote attention to the phone conversation occurring on the other side of the couch. But she enjoyed that level of control only through the first half of the exchange, the pressure building to where Aria silently begged Jack to get the fuck off the phone so that she could avoid ruining the most comfortable couch on the planet. By then any words she heard were being filtered through a curtain of urine and stress. By then Aria comprehended that Jack was speaking, but not that the words had separate sound and meaning, similar to the incomprehensible drone of a beehive.

Finally, the mind/body struggle came to a head, and she leapt off the couch as from an ejector seat, and rushed past Jack without explanation. There would be plenty of time to explain *after*. Despite Aria's pressing need and accompanying inability to discern individual words in her native language, she did manage to comprehend the sentence that came out of Jack's mouth just as she ran past.

"Can I bring a friend?"

This made her happy.

I've gotta be the "friend," right?

Jack hung up the phone right after Aria dove into the bathroom and waited for her to emerge before passing along what he suspected she already knew.

"That was my dad."

Aria nodded. "Yeah. Are you ok?"

Free Will

Jack allowed the question to sink in. "I think so?" He was staring out the window. "Listen, do you want to get out of here for a few minutes? Take a walk?"

Aria took Jack's hand and chose not to comment on his penchant for walking to clear his mind. "Maybe grab a cup of coffee?"

"Ha. Okay, yes, you're really funny."

"Just so you know, it's your turn." She pointed to the coffee table. "I wrote while you were tripping around the neighborhood without me."

Jack glanced at the notebook and was intrigued by what he might find from Aria but, after the conversation with his father, was equally anxious to take some notes, while it was still fresh in his mind.

"Do you mind if I read it now?"

"Of course not. I need time to fix my hair, anyway."

The comment prompted Jack to look at Aria's hair in a more critical light, and it reminded him of the bare-legged girl from the coffee shop that morning. Her thick locks seemed to have lost their structural integrity, slumping to one side of her head and obscuring that side of her face. She smiled at him while she attempted, unsuccessfully, to center it back on top of her skull. Jack nearly laughed, unable to take his eyes off of her. He was sure he'd never seen anything quite so lovely.

As Aria departed to tame her unruly locks, Jack sat down on the couch, the cushion still warm from her body heat. It took him no time to read her entry and begin writing his own.

2:09 PM

Man! You sure do have a lot of thoughts on books, bookshelves, and the relationship between them. I have to say I've never thought of them quite in the way you describe, which is wonderful.

Even from an engineering perspective. Especially from an engineering perspective.
I'll think more about it, and we can share our ideas.
I don't know how much you heard when I was talking to my dad.
He invited me over for dinner, and I want you to go. I need you to go.
You don't have to, of course.
Neither do I, now that I think about it. Free will and all that. I/we can do what we want.
In fact, there's a lot I don't think I have to do now. Not anymore.
Even so, I AM going to the dinner. Because I want to. Not because I feel obligated.
And speaking of getting what you want, it looks like you might be getting your wish.
The one about me reconnecting with my family, I mean.
Although I think the reconnecting part remains to be seen, outside of my dad.
I honestly have no idea what to expect. I don't know who'll be there.
It might just be Mom and Dad, but I feel like Dad's got something bigger planned.
It would be great to have you there. You could distract some attention away from me.
I'll tell you I've felt like I've been flailing around the past year. Lost. You know?
I feel like all I've been doing is getting by, doing only what I needed to get through the day.

But I don't have to do that anymore. Not now. Not after last night and today.

No pressure, but you've changed everything.

Jack felt Aria's arms curl around him from the back of the couch. He closed the notebook and set it down.

"Were you able to see what I was writing?" He hoped she had, hoped she'd been there longer than he'd realized.

"No. I'll read it later. Did you want to bring it with us?" Aria's lips were only a few inches from his ear, making it difficult for Jack to string thoughts together. He managed an answer as Aria released him from the embrace.

"I'm okay with leaving it here. Less chance of losing it. I've already lost one today. I really want to keep this one." He almost finished the sentence with "because you're in it" but thought it sounded too gooey.

"Makes sense. Let's get out of here."

The world Aria and Jack stepped into was noticeably different from the one in which they arrived at the condo that morning. Above them the sun was poking through the clouds; below them, sidewalks were beginning to appear as the snow slowly melted. It was easier to walk in this changed environment. It was easier to see where they were going.

Without a word, Aria led them toward the river, feeling pulled in that direction. It was also conveniently downhill, mostly. Jack did not object, and regardless had put little thought into their direction. It just seemed natural to walk south, to walk downhill. They walked hand-in-hand, now much warmer and more comfortable than during their earlier excursions. This time even their feet were dry, and their clothing actually fit. To the casual observer, they blended perfectly into the urban landscape through which they moved, but there was no escaping the eagle-eyed reporter who was hot on their trail.

River Van Beek was in the middle of a sip of coffee when he saw the couple come around the corner of the orange building. He nearly spilled it on his shirt, though he wouldn't have cared. He was too excited to cry over spilt coffee. Gathering his personal and professional items yet again, he positioned himself by the door, stood with as much nonchalance as he could muster, and waited.

When River felt his quarry had travelled just the right amount of distance down the street, he slung his canvas bag over his shoulder and pushed through the door to the sidewalk. River gratefully took note of the pace. As a couple, Jack and Aria moved more leisurely than had Jack as a single, and the pace steadier, as if they knew where they were going but were in no rush to get there. River fell in behind them and was hopeful his heart rate wouldn't be called upon to spike from extra effort.

But the best part was that, this time, he was absolutely sure he was following the right people. River felt like he recognized the couple, like maybe he'd seen them somewhere together that day, and though this recognition was mostly subconscious, it strengthened the voice in his head, the encouraging voice that told him he was finally on the right track. And the voice said something else. It told River he could stop questioning his career choice.

River walked with a smile, his first of the day.

Jack and Aria strolled down the wet sidewalks, inexorably propelled toward the river. They spoke little, occasionally noting the landmarks from the night before, landmarks hardly noticed until now. Everything looked different in the daylight, *sans* snowstorm. Less ominous. They were familiar with the buildings, had walked or driven past them for years, sometimes aware of them, mostly not, busy moving from one place to the next with little consideration for the in-between.

Now, however, the buildings were almost breathing, almost alive, as if they might answer if questioned. Neither had before experienced the city in quite this way. They felt they were on vacation, with the luxury of time to examine their surroundings, to be astounded by the effort and thought manifested in this feature or that. Before long they began to point out architectural details to each other, saying things like, "Look at that," or "Isn't that called dentil molding?" and then respond with "Yeah, wow," or "I think you're right. It definitely looks like teeth."

They arrived at the corner, at Central Parkway, the border between their historic neighborhood and downtown. Cars, which had been rare earlier in the day, when they first encountered River in the coffee shop, were now moving steadily up and down the mostly snow-free pavement. Jack and Aria stood hand in hand, staring in the direction of the river, still nearly a mile away, obscured by the buildings of the city center. When the light changed, each waited for the other to move, to take the first step off the curb, but neither seemed willing. Indeed, they stood, almost trance-like, until the walk light implored them to cross the invisible threshold.

River was pleased at how easily he was able to keep pace with Jack and Aria, and wondered if it was possible that his physical condition had somehow improved over the last few hours. After all, what else could explain the ease with which he now kept up with two people in a clearly superior state of fitness? He made sure to keep a safe distance, and was pleased there were more people on the street than when he'd followed Jack. The extra bodies helped him blend into the background, an ability he'd mastered during puberty.

River had fallen into a steady pace, only occasionally feeling the need to mark the distance between him and the couple-with-a-story he was following. His breathing was as even as the pace and he, like Jack and Aria, found himself noticing the historic architecture with which he was surrounded. He progressed unimpeded, at least until met with an immovable object.

Umph!

River gasped for breath. He'd been staring up at the roof lines of the buildings across the street, the distraction causing him to veer off course. He didn't notice the sturdy pole of the street sign until contact. Luckily for River, his plump torso took most of the force of the blow, leaving his head and face mostly undamaged.

Shaken, but undeterred by the pole encounter, River checked on the progress of his targets. Luckily for him, it appeared they'd stopped moving, and were standing perfectly still on the corner.

River decided to suspend his forward motion as well, ducking into an alley so as not to appear too conspicuous. From the alley, he spied them from around the corner and was sure he'd not been noticed, which pleased him. A minute later, when he peeked around the corner again, Jack and Aria had seemingly teleported to the opposite side of Central Parkway, and River was back to playing catch up.

The spike in heart rate now all too familiar, he accepted it as just another job hazard, even as he hoped that if he *did* have a heart attack, someone close by would have the presence of mind to call an ambulance.

John Current hung up the phone, barely able to contain himself, sure he would explode with joy. He was so sure he would explode with joy that he put his fingers on his carotid artery to check his pulse. It was elevated, as would be expected for anyone who was in danger of exploding. John sat down and started making a list of the things he needed to accomplish before seven o'clock. It was not a long list, but the first item did nothing to slow his heart rate. He would have to tell Susan what he'd done.

Chapter Fourteen

Bridging the Divide

Jack and Aria took the moment on the corner to look south and wait for the light to change. Although they didn't know it, this was the point at which their paths converged the night before, just minutes apart. While they had talked about what each had experienced before they found each other on the bridge, they hadn't had the time or inclination to map out their individual tours of the neighborhood. Together now, they didn't know how close they'd come to running into each other after they left Liberty's. Or how many times. They *would* find out later, however, and have a good laugh, with plenty of oohs and aahs.

For now, Jack and Aria focused on the path in front of them, overlooking the brown-suited bumbler following behind, even when their stalker ran into a sign pole, thereby releasing a more-than-noticeable grunt from the involuntarily expelled air from his lungs. In fact, they might not have noticed him even had the sign pole collision occurred twenty feet in *front* of them. Though they enjoyed taking in the surroundings as they ambled toward the river, toward the scene of the "crime," their thoughts became more internalized with every step.

Above them the cloud cover continued to dissipate; beneath them the snow continued to melt. The temperature, now above freezing, would soon render Jack and Aria's outer jackets superfluous, though not quite yet. There was still a chill in the air, and they enjoyed the warmth of their clothing.

Jack found it impossible to shut off the replay of the conversation he'd had with his father and it nearly drove him to distraction. He was happy he made the call, overjoyed really, but knew there was much left to say. This was doubly true if his mother, Susan, were involved which, of course, she would be. There was no way Jack's father was going to undertake a reunion of this magnitude without the knowledge of his wife. Jack did not envy his father in this regard, and wondered if he'd already broken the news to her. The thought made Jack nervous. And worried.

Aria walked next to Jack, holding his hand, untortured by his racing thoughts. She didn't have the full story of Jack's familial history, and her ignorance of the family dynamic allowed her the freedom to stroll along thinking only good thoughts, happy she'd somehow played a positive role in the pending summit. Or perhaps it was more an intervention? It didn't matter. Aria believed a reconciliation was overdue, and was downright excited to be a part of it. At that moment she believed everything was possible, that everything would work out. She believed—no, *knew*—the sun was shining just for them. It was their day. They'd survived the crucible together. They'd earned a happy ending. She was sure of it.

Aria didn't mention any of this to Jack. She didn't want to jinx it. She would bide her time, stand with him for the rest of this day and (hopefully) many more, and watch as things fell into place. But she wasn't going to tell him that. She didn't want him to think her insane. After all, they'd just started dating, and though it was by far the strangest, most intense date she'd ever experienced, it was still too soon to release what her friend Tracy referred to as "the crazy," though Aria preferred to think of it as "insane optimism."

"How are you doing? Are your legs holding up?"

Jack's voice startled her from her rumination on their future together, but Aria managed a cogent response.

"Good, good. Can't even tell I fell off a bridge last night."

"Or crawled out of a river."

Jack laughed and she laughed with him. They were bonded. They'd shared an experience like no other, one that wouldn't be forgotten, no matter what the future held.

The buildings surrounded them. Granite was everywhere. Red, brown, black, gray. If you looked closely, you could see the variously-hued crystalline flecks that composed the ubiquitous stone. Aria had never really noticed before, but even the curbs were made of granite. She wondered how old they must be. The "cobblestone era?" There were still a few cobblestone streets in the historic neighborhood. Weren't they granite, too? This thought was immediately followed by another.

"Any idea how much granite there is in the world?"

"Let me guess. You're looking at the curbs and thinking there must be a shitload of granite in the world if we can afford to use it as curbs."

Aria giggled. "Yeah. Good guess. But it doesn't answer my question."

"Great question. Don't really know. A shitload?" Jack paused. "Yeah, 'shitload' sounds about right. There are whole mountains of it."

Aria allowed her mind to dwell on granite. She needed a bit of a distraction, lest her giddy optimism reveal itself prematurely. She began to wonder from where it came, how it formed. Did all those colors come from different places? Not being a granite expert, she thought about asking Jack, but wasn't sure his state of mind was amenable to an in-depth discussion of what appeared to be nearly indestructible stone. No, she was pretty sure his thoughts had returned to his family, returned to the excitement and trepidation he'd been feeling since she made him listen to his father's message.

But she couldn't stop thinking about granite. *Ooh! Another curb!* Aria decided she needed to climb out of the granite-lined rabbit hole into which she'd fallen. She could study up on another day. This day was to be spent with her arms out, ready to catch Jack at a moment's notice, should the need arise. She would be his granite, she told herself. Indestructible. Multi-hued. Multi-faceted. She liked the thought.

Jack *was* thinking about his family, wondering what would befall him a few hours hence, once he reentered his parents' home. He couldn't stop thinking about it. Couldn't stop fretting. Aria's intrusion into these thoughts, with her curiosity concerning one particular type of construction material, was welcome. Their short interaction offered him the opportunity to think about something else; it allowed him not to dread the feelings with which he was dealing. And granite talk was right up his alley. Jack could talk about granite for hours, given the chance. But Aria's curiosity seemed to have moved on. Perhaps another day . . .

Suddenly, Jack was feeling inadequate as Aria's boyfriend. There he was, he told himself, walking along, obsessing over seeing his parents later that day, having completely forgotten about the invitation to drinks with *Aria's* parents. The thought of it had gotten lost in the mental ruckus that ensued after speaking with his father.

Should I tell her we should cancel my parents?

No, he told himself. They could certainly do both. Drinks and then more drinks. Maybe some food in the mix. No sleep, of course. Jack smiled, thinking they still had plenty of Modafinil left over from their excursion to the hospital pharmacy. The drug had treated them well thus far, and Jack trusted it would continue to do so. If it didn't, there was no way either one of them was going to make it through the evening.

"Remember this place?" Aria nodded toward the Main Event. "I wasn't far behind you when I got here last night."

Free Will

Jack certainly remembered. The Main Event was the scene of his *second* bar brawl the night before (both involuntary) as well as his clandestine escape from Kevin.

"Your friend really helped me out. You know, I mean when it came to finding you last night."

Jack understood she was referring to Kevin, whom he'd schemed, successfully, to leave behind in the Main Event, using the brawl as a means of escape. Now, however, he wanted to give him a hug, perhaps buy him another beer. After all, he thought, he kind of owed Kevin his life.

Had Kevin not been there to point Aria in my direction, I would have gone off the bridge on my own.

He thought about that potentiality, and it occurred to him, now that he'd actually survived the fall, it was likely he would have survived with or without Aria. It also occurred to him that things on the bridge hadn't really worked out for Aria, whose only intention was to keep him from jumping. It seemed to Jack, then, that the survival problem wasn't so much a function of the company one had on the bridge, or who went with who into the water. More likely, he thought, the bridge just wasn't high enough off the water to induce the necessary trauma. Certainly not high enough for maximum impact. Of course, there was always the hypothermia . . .

Shut up! Shut up! Shut up! What are you doing, dumbass?

Jack pushed the thought out of his head, knowing it was ridiculous to dwell on such things, especially considering he had no intention of putting the theory to the test.

"I definitely owe Kevin a beer. Maybe even two beers. If it hadn't been for him, I'd have been all alone in the water."

Aria laughed. So far she'd expended little effort to dwell on the circumstances of her own plunge. She, of course, understood the facts, understood the events leading up to the moment she went over the railing, but those events were already turning hazy, as if it had been months, not hours, since the fall.

Nor had she taken much time to deliberate the mystery of those events. Was Kevin's role in her unplanned swim coincidence or fate?

Hmm . . .

She pondered the moment, then decided to leave that existential question to another day. She already had plenty with which to deal on this one.

Aria returned to enjoying her surroundings. They were now well past the Main Event, and getting close to the Bay Horse, its neon sign floating over the sidewalk.

"Speaking of beers . . ." Aria pointed them toward the saloon, smiling at the memory of finally being able to apologize to Brian for the pain her youthful indiscretion had caused him in high school. "Feel like having one?"

It was hard for Jack to say no. Being the last bar on his suicidal crawl through the city, and the last place he made an entry in the original drunk log, he couldn't help but have sentimental feelings for the Bay Horse, to attach a certain significance to the place.

"Or we could do shots."

Aria nodded in agreement. Under the circumstances shots seemed fitting, and not only from the standpoint of misplaced nostalgia. She had a practical reason. Drinking shots took less time than drinking beer, and they had plans for the evening.

River watched Jack and Aria duck into the Bay Horse. It made him anxious. He did not relish the idea of standing around on the sidewalk in the cold while those two sat on comfortable barstools and sipped drinks in a climate-controlled environment. But what choice did he have? He couldn't just wander in, belly up to the bar, and have a drink himself. In fact, River had never been much of a drinker, being one of those rare individuals who just never found a taste for it. But, luckily for him, he'd been invited to few parties while in college, or since, so peer pressure had never been a problem.

He decided to stick it out, crossing his fingers they wouldn't linger over their drinks. Though the snow was melting, what was left was beginning to seep into his street shoes, chilling his feet. His shoes now damp, they began to squeak with every step.

Luckily, River didn't have to wait long, and he was pleased with the efficiency with which Jack and Aria were able to drink. They left the bar within minutes of arriving and, as he watched, headed south. They did not notice him hovering a block away, hiding in the doorway of an office supply store. River followed, hoping the mouse-like squeaks coming from the wet leather of his shoes would go unnoticed.

Jack and Aria were still a couple blocks away when the bridge first presented itself, the tops of the towers rising behind the buildings lining the streets in front of them. From where they stood, they could see snow still clinging to the rock on the north faces of the two towers which, along with the sweeping curves of the blue steel suspension system, stood out in high relief against the low angle of the November sun. As they drew closer to the span, they could hear the open steel of the deck "sing" as cars passed back and forth between Ohio and Kentucky, the cities on both sides of the river now back to life after the unexpected storm.

Part of Jack dreaded the return. Part of him felt no need to ever see the bridge again, though he knew that was unrealistic. There was really no way for him *never* to see it again, not unless he discovered some miraculous way of moving around the city, one that included trips to the dry cleaner, running shoe shop, or favorite liquor store, all of which were located on the Kentucky side of the river. He supposed he could find a new liquor store, and maybe even a new running shoe shop, but the dry cleaner was another issue. He would be hard-pressed to find one as good as the one he'd been using for years, and so resigned himself to reality. There was no way to avoid using—or at least seeing—the bridge in his day-to-day existence. He would just have to live with it. He supposed he could leave town altogether, but rejected the idea out of hand. The last thing he wanted was to find another dry cleaner, no matter where he might land.

Aria, on the other hand, could barely contain her excitement. Unlike Jack, she viewed the bridge as one piece of a larger triumph, that triumph being the saving of Jack from a watery death. Though unable to avoid the glaring detail that she and Jack still ended up in the river, she chose to embrace the positive. They'd survived and if, in the universe, there was anything resembling a "plan," then she and Jack were clearly meant for something more. They had to be, she thought, or else they wouldn't have *both* survived. Together.

She sensed, however, that Jack did not share her current level of enthusiasm, and so kept a lid on it, at least for the moment.

Aria understood, of course, her premise was likely full of crap. The chances of a universal "plan" hardly seemed plausible. Still, she refused to allow the plausibility of a plan, or lack thereof, to stop her from feeling hopeful, to feel she could do more than just stand by and watch things happen randomly around her. She felt powerful. She had done for Jack what she couldn't do for Steffi, a thought that kept her joy in check. She couldn't go back in time; she couldn't change anything that had happened before that moment. She knew that but knowing it didn't stop her from wanting it.

Unexpectedly, a sense of dread replaced Aria's covert joy.

Free Will

Would he try again?

Aria looked up at Jack's face, trying to read his thoughts.

She didn't think so. Not really. Not after everything.

But what if she was wrong? What if the call from his father had the effect opposite the one she believed it had, opposite the one she'd hoped for? Mostly, she didn't think it was possible, didn't believe everything she'd experienced with Jack could lead to another swim. Still...

"What's going through *your* head right now?" Aria's inflection was one of like-minded companionship. She wanted to let him know he wasn't alone should his thoughts be migrating to the negative, that she was there with him. His granite.

She was pleased with his answer.

"Actually, I was just thinking about how stupid I was yesterday, and how lucky I am today."

What Jack was feeling could best be described as relief. Or maybe bliss. Or a combination of the two. Relief his plan had failed. Bliss that Aria had cared enough to follow him. Relief he hadn't killed her in the process. Bliss that he was around to return his dad's call that morning. And the feeling was growing. He couldn't stop it. It was beyond his control. In fact, by the time he and Aria stepped onto the bridge, he felt his heart might actually burst.

In a good way, he thought.

Still, he was 79% sure his heart wouldn't *actually* burst. For now, he decided, he would just let the mania run its course, and see how it ended, and *if* it ended. If he had a choice, and he wasn't absolutely sure he did, he believed he was making the right one.

Jack squeezed Aria's hand as they marched toward the north tower, silently retracing their steps from the night before and silently reliving it—as if in a movie playing only for them, one in which they played the only parts.

They stopped when they reached the place they'd gone over the rail, wordlessly acknowledging the location. Still silent, they stepped to the rail and peered over the edge into the churning water below. The distance to the surface was not as far as they remembered, the river below not as threatening in the light of day. But Jack did not feel completely relieved. Something was crawling up his spine—the stark realization that just hours before he'd tried to kill himself. His legs gone weak, he managed to step back from the rail and stabilize himself with his back to the immovable rock of the north tower.

Aria stepped back to Jack and took his hand, opting for hopeful humor over dread. "I think we'd still make it, you know, if we really wanted a re-do." Aria forced a laugh as she stared at his face.

Jack, staring over the rail, forced a laugh in return. "Agreed. I really didn't plan this very well, did I?"

River stared with a sort of trepidation as the couple walked hand in hand out to the walkway around the north tower, somehow simultaneously fearful *and* hopeful they might try again. He didn't wish them ill. Not really. But he'd found himself in the middle of a delusion of grandeur, one he'd been cultivating since seeing the bridge. The delusion went something like this:

Intrepid reporter is tailing a young couple who may, or may not, have intended to do themselves harm. Intrepid reporter is, initially, on the sidelines, so to speak, watching the young couple from a short distance away. Due to the reporter's amazing skills, the young couple, quite naturally, have no idea they're being followed.

Intrepid reporter watches as the lovers, distraught and inconsolable, walk to the railing of the bridge walkway. Holding hands, they stare out over the river, its vast, unstoppable flow an analogy for life itself. They are lost in the contemplation of their last minutes on this earth.

Finally, in a moment of unspoken, mutual agreement, they each release the hand of the other and climb over the rail. On the other side, their hands rejoin.

They jump.

The dauntless reporter, bearing witness to this tragedy, gathers his strength and runs, not toward the bridge, but to the shoreline past it. He's running so fast he can see the heads of the lovers bobbing along as he passes them. Finally, and with Herculean effort, the stalwart reporter makes his move. They drift close to shore, he dives into the icy water, grabbing both victims of despair by their coat collars. With whatever strength remains in him, he drags them to shore, snatching them from the jaws of a frigid death.

A hero is born.

Given the power of River's delusion, and desire for a breakout story, especially one in which he plays a central role, it was not surprising he was disappointed when Jack and Aria turned back, away from the rail. Unbeknownst to him, they'd gone exactly as far as they needed to go, and no further. They'd taken time to gaze upon the parts of the bridge and river they were unable to see fifteen hours earlier, in the darkness of midnight, and were satisfied. For now, anyway.

River could know none of this. He was not privy to their conversation on the bridge nor, indeed, any of their conversations at all, and as he watched them walk back toward his hiding place behind one of the massive, stone cable anchorages, he fell into a panic. The hunter had become . . . well, not the hunted, per se. But, certainly, the tables had turned and the last thing he wanted was to be spotted by his quarry, even if they had no idea who he was or what he wanted. The big reveal, he believed, would happen sometime later, at a time and a place of his choosing, once he had the story in order.

River, in the process of slinking backward, was quite nearly flattened by a car circling the roundabout at the end of the bridge. But the wail of a car horn averted the collision, and the answering scream from River let the driver know the errant pedestrian was adequately humbled by his stupidity. With little choice, River used the near-death experience to facilitate his escape, walking as briskly as possible back up Walnut Street, again hoping his presence had not been noted by the couple he'd been tailing.

He very quickly found himself out of breath. It was uphill, after all.

"Did you see that?" Aria tugged at the arm of Jack's winter coat. "That guy almost got run over. Did you hear him scream?"

Jack squinted to get a closer look at the roundabout, but had not witnessed the man vs. machine near miss. He did, however, hear the scream, and saw the dumpy man in a trench coat making labored progress up the steep grade of Walnut Street.

Jack recognized him from earlier. The man from Coffee Emporium. The Mad Knocker. His marginally surreptitious tail.

"I think that's our new friend."

John Current decided there was no time like the present, and marched out of the kitchen to find his wife, who happened to be folding laundry in the bedroom. It had been a long time since he'd felt fear, but John felt it now as he described his morning to Susan, described everything he thought and felt and how he couldn't hold it in any longer. Susan sat on the edge of the bed, listening politely, tears streaming.

Chapter Fifteen

Fortune Favors the Bold

The walk back was uphill, at least the first few blocks. Neither Jack nor Aria found it particularly enjoyable, their legs still spent from their night-before excursions, their subsequent escape from the river, the running around in the hospital, and the sheer exhaustion that accompanied having been (mostly) awake for more than a day.

They held hands, each either pulling or being pulled uphill by the other at any given time. Jack, especially, was anxious to catch up to the man in the trench coat, wondered again why he was following them, why he'd been following them all day. Who was he? Jack toyed with the question as they waited for the walk signal on Fourth Street. He thought it likely he was a compatriot of Deputy Lane, their tormentor from the riverbank and hospital. Who else would have known where to go looking for them? Who else would have had Jack's address? And why wouldn't Lane just have stayed on the clock? Was *he* too tired after the long night in the hospital? But the guy didn't look like a cop. At all. Plainclothes detective?

Jack dismissed the idea somewhere in the middle of the crosswalk, deciding it unlikely Lane had anything to do with the Mad Knocker. Hell, he'd actually given them a ride home from the hospital that very morning. This didn't seem the behavior of someone interested in "taking you down." No. Trench-coat-guy clearly had his own motivations. But what were they?

"Who do you think that guy is?"

Aria gave it a moment of thought. "Friend of Lane's?"

"I thought that too, but now I'm thinking no. I think Lane gave up trying to pin anything on us. Any other ideas?"

As they waited for the next green light, Aria's brain shifted into overdrive. If not Lane, then who? What was it about the two of them that was so interesting it was worth spending the day hunting them down? She created a short list of possibilities. Private detective? Distant relative who wanted to let Aria know her late Aunt Sally left her a ton of money? Process server? reporter?

"Reporter" quickly gained traction. It made sense. There would be a police report, and a reporter could have read it and pursued the story.

"He's gotta be a reporter," she decided.

"Really?"

"Think about it. What makes *us* so fascinating? I mean, let's face it, we're not that special, except for what happened to us on the bridge. It's the only thing that sets us apart from anybody else on the street. Last night, we were the ones who fell off the bridge."

Jack felt the need to correct her. "Well, one of us, you, fell. The other one, me, jumped in to save you."

Aria laughed. "Yeah, but we told everybody we fell on the ice. The cops, the nurses, the doctors. We told them all the same thing. Bad lie or not, people don't fall off that bridge every day, and that makes us newsworthy. Don't you think?"

Jack found Aria's logic unassailable. Of course, he thought, the chubby guy in the ill-fitting suit and rumpled trench coat *had* to be a reporter. What else could he be? But the idea begged another question.

Jack looked down at Aria. "Okay, then why did he run away when he saw us? Why didn't he just walk up and start asking questions?"

"Good question. Maybe he was trying to catch us in the act?"

"In the act of what, exactly? Does he think we're going to jump off the damn bridge *again*?"

Aria chose not to mention she'd had the same fear earlier that day. "Not sure. Maybe. Or maybe he's just not very good at his job."

River scurried up the sidewalk as fast as he could, trying not to allow the thumping in his chest to slow him down. He wanted to get away from the bridge as quickly as possible, as he was fairly certain Jack and Aria spotted him right before he was nearly plastered by the oncoming car. It occurred to him, as he struggled for breath, that he may as well have introduced himself when he had the chance. After all, he'd bruised his knuckles rapping on their apartment door earlier that morning. If he was ready to talk to them at that point, what was stopping him now?

River, once he felt he'd put enough distance between himself and the couple, slowed his pace to think about the question. One answer was obvious—he started the day with nothing more than two names and a vague description of the jumpers. He owed it to his readers (though admittedly small in number) to identify the subjects of his story before he approached them. There was also fear, he realized. But fear of what?

Maybe, he thought, there was something in him that just didn't want the story to be over. And if there was a story, it was definitely the best story he'd ever been given the chance to tell.

But, still, why not just talk to them? What had his lurking accomplished thus far? The obvious answer, even for River, was nothing. He vowed to speak with them at the very next opportunity, but failed to recognize this *was* the next opportunity. All he had to do was turn around, walk a few blocks south and introduce himself to Jack and Aria. Instead, he decided to gather a little more information. He just needed to figure out what information required gathering.

River quickened his pace and headed for the coffee shop. Surely, the barista could give him some "color" on Jack and Aria. He wondered why he hadn't asked already.

Tracy did not feel good about leaving her friend alone with Jack. Admittedly, his demeanor, at least in her presence, was *not* that of a serial killer or kidnapper, though she admitted to herself she had no idea what the demeanors of serial killers or kidnappers might be. But his story frightened her. Aria's sister, Steffi, was the only person she'd ever known to have killed herself, and that was what frightened her about Jack. Sure, he seemed calm and rational when they were all in his apartment together, but she carried sharp memories of Steffi's erratic behavior, how she could create a tornado out of a sunny day. It could happen in an instant. Tracy wondered if Jack was the same; she wondered if his earlier demeanor was just the calm before the storm. That's why, after checking in with her husband, she jumped in her car and headed back downtown. She needed to know Aria was safe. She needed to see it for herself.

It was, perhaps, her intense preoccupation with the well-being of her best friend that allowed Tracy to miss seeing Aria and Jack walking north in the melting snow. But it wasn't just her light obsession with her friend and her friend's new boyfriend distracting her. It was the string of green lights stretching out in front of her, into the horizon. She couldn't remember anything like it ever happening and was surprised it was even possible. She was clearly in a window of traffic flow serendipity. She came close to braking more than once, but before she was forced to touch the pedal, the light miraculously turned from red to green. Every time. Tracy almost called her husband to tell him what was happening, but was afraid to upset the balance, afraid to take her attention from the phenomenon she was experiencing, lest the distraction alter the immediate alchemy of the universe.

Though in the "zone," Tracy did notice a hefty man in a brown trench coat. It was likely she noticed him because he was so obviously struggling to make it up the sidewalk. She had no idea who he was, and in passing thought he might be homeless. She dismissed the theory as she slipped through yet another green light. His garb was at least one step above that of the panhandlers she was used to seeing downtown.

Tracy pulled into a parking space in front of Liberty's, having miraculously hit twelve green lights in a row. Engine off, she sat motionless, allowing the wonder of it to pass through her body. She was sure the twelve green lights were a portent of good things to come, a sign the day had shifted for the better. Her good fortune, however, also brought doubts. She now suspected she'd driven back downtown for no reason, that her friend would be just fine without her. But she was now, pleasantly, child-free. And she'd already carved out the afternoon for her personal use. And she wanted a glass of wine. Tracy pulled her phone from her purse.

"I'm at Liberty's. Meet me for a drink."

Aria felt her phone vibrate against her thigh, though she had no desire to answer it. She was enjoying the walk with Jack. Unlike most of her friends, Aria had developed a kind of immunity to the tempting immediacy of a buzzing pocket, and the fact she often left her phone unanswered frustrated those same friends. So, she left the phone in her pocket, firm in her conviction that whatever was being texted could certainly wait until they made it back to Jack's condo.

Jack's condo. This made her think. Had she already reached a level of comfort where the thought of going to Jack's place felt more natural than the thought of going to hers? They were, at that moment, passing her building. It was right across the street. Aria's mind shifted up. Did she have everything she needed for the evening? Was there something she wanted? What was she forgetting?

Think, think, think . . .

"Jack, do you mind if we stop in at my place for a minute? I need a few things for . . . later."

Aria really had no clue as to what she thought she needed or didn't need, had remembered or forgotten. She relied instead on a belief that whatever she needed would be revealed, so long as she was standing before it. Separate from that belief, it occurred to Aria she might be getting a little pushy. After all, they'd just started "dating" the night before. Despite everything they'd been through, despite all the shared joy and trauma, they were still "new." Maybe he wasn't ready to welcome another bag of her belongings into his foyer. Maybe his brain hadn't caught up to hers in this matter. But Aria's fears were quickly allayed.

"Sure. No problem. Get whatever you need."

Jack actually found the idea of Aria bringing more items to his household intriguing, and not frightening in a way it might have been just a day or two earlier. Simultaneously, he felt no desire to step across her threshold until a team of highly trained sterilization personnel were given the opportunity to scour her apartment. He would do it if he had to, for Aria, he just wouldn't like it. He walked across the street with her and stopped at the entrance door.

"You don't need to come in, Jack. I'll only be a second. I know what I want." Even though Aria did not yet know what specific items she desired from her apartment, she *was* sure she didn't want Jack in her apartment. The experience of his first visit horrified her, and she had no desire to relive it. She would spend tomorrow cleaning. "Why don't you stay out here and enjoy the sunshine."

Jack's relief was palpable, and he did not bother to feign an objection.

"I'll be right here."

Aria left Jack on the street and climbed the steps to her apartment. To her dismay and disappointment, the place looked exactly as she'd left it. Sadly, the cleaning fairies had not worked their magic in her absence.

Tomorrow. You'll take care of it tomorrow. Just grab your stuff.

It was immediately apparent that Aria's assumption that the needed items would simply call out "take me" was not working out. Nothing jumped out at her. Nothing. Not wanting to have wasted the time, she grabbed a spacious shoulder bag and began, for want of a better word, "shopping." A pair of clean panties and a bra. The basics were always a good place to start. She located those items at the bottom of a pile of clean (she assumed) laundry sitting on top of the dryer. For good measure, she threw in a pair of jeans, socks and a T-shirt, and some toiletries which had yet to escape the bathroom. But she wasn't finished.

River watched the couple from behind the corner of a building a block away, noting Jack did not enter with Aria. He wondered if Jack was standing watch, but couldn't figure out exactly *why* he would be standing watch. Jack looked tired, or bored, or perhaps both, and these things River was feeling as well. He'd had a long day, and wanted to resolve all this in one way or another.

But how?

His recliner and television beckoned, but he wasn't ready to walk away, at least not yet. So, he told himself, he needed to finish the story. To do that, he would have to undertake some sort of bold action. He would have to do something to complete it one way or another. He would have to do something big. Maybe even something dangerous.

Adrenaline pumped through River, and the idea of being bold, of being courageous, for real this time, became ever more plausible. But what would it be? His thoughts and heart racing, River took some deep breaths and allowed his frontal lobe to unclench itself.

What would Bob do?

His brain gave him two options. He could either walk straight up to Jack and Aria, introduce himself, and hope they were open to an interview. Or he could break into Jack's condo and sniff around for clues. Admittedly, he had no idea what kind of clues he'd be looking for, but it would save him from actually having to confront Jack and Aria.

River made his decision, knowing it was the bolder of the two choices. He would confront them, face to face. Damn the torpedoes.

He returned to his perch at the coffee shop, and waited.

Given the chaos of Aria's apartment, a more organized person would surely be surprised at how quickly she was able to locate the items she'd put in her bag. Aria seemed to know exactly where everything was located, as if she'd created a map or arranged the place in a way only she could understand. Things were strewn about, often having no logical relationship to their proximate neighbors, but this did not seem to matter to Aria. She located an eyeliner on one of the kitchen counters, where it was living next to the toothbrush she used to scrub the hard-to-reach places in pots and pans. Her actual toothbrush, the one she used on her teeth, resided on the soap shelf in the shower, right next to an open bottle of conditioner and a disposable razor.

She wandered the apartment like a bumble bee, gathering items and stuffing them into the bag. She wondered how the place had gotten to such a state. This was not the first time Aria had pondered this, but now the situation seemed more consequential—she now had someone she wanted to have over, someone for whom she did not want to appear deranged.

Before long, she found herself making piles of this and that, clearing this surface or that, but before long realized now was not the time for it. She had someone waiting for her on the sidewalk below; someone she'd told not to come in. He was her responsibility and it was wrong of her to leave him standing in the cold.

Aria glanced around one more time before walking out the door with her bag of goodies. She triaged the items she could see, identifying what needed to be cleaned first and what could wait. All she had to do was find the time to do it, reckoning it would not be that weekend. They were already exhausted and, should they survive the rest of their day, they would need to sleep, finally, on Sunday.

Not just sleep, she smiled to herself. After all, they *were* "new."

Either way, she made sure she took enough spare clothing for another day or two. She would start cleaning before her next shift, before she went back to the remnants of her old life, the residue of which now seemed impossibly far away. The thought struck her as she joined Jack on the sidewalk. After the last twenty-four hours, how could her life go back to what it had been the day before? It couldn't, she decided easily. And that was ok. She was sure today was better than yesterday; absolutely sure the universe had thrown all this at her, at them, to see what they would do with it.

Aria slipped the bag back over her shoulder and, finding him waiting patiently by the door, took Jack's hand.

"You ready? We've got a big evening, don't we?"

Jack squeezed her hand in affirmation as they started to walk. As they approached Liberty's, Aria recognized the blue BMW parked in front of the bar.

"Hmmm . . . That's weird."

"What's weird?"

"Tracy's here."

Their pace neither slowed or quickened, each figuring Tracy's car wasn't going anywhere and, even if it was, it didn't matter. Tracy's presence, however, did alter their plans. A nap, of any length was now, most likely, out of the question. Tracy's reappearance was certainly no coincidence. She was there for them. They just weren't sure why.

Once again ensconced in the coffee shop across from Liberty's, River took a few minutes to question the barista on any information he might have concerning Jack and Aria. None was forthcoming. This was only his third shift and, as far as he knew, neither of them had ever bought coffee from him. Now, sitting back in the window, River watched Jack and Aria cross the street and enter the bar. His first instinct, something he'd learned never to trust, was to jump up and follow them in. Because of this distrust, he decided to give them a few minutes to settle in. He then gathered his reporting *accoutrements* one last time, wished the barista well, and left the coffee shop for good.

Tracy watched Jack and Aria walking hand in hand and smiled. She had always felt protective of her friend, and still wasn't quite sure what to think of the new boyfriend, but she felt better than she had the night before. The green lights had seen to that. She knew as well that even after Aria fell off the curb and bloodied her face, there was no way to stop her from doing what she wanted. It had always been thus, and Tracy wasn't going to fight it now. Who was she to tell Aria how to live her life? No, on the drive back she'd decided to embrace them both, or at least try to embrace them both. Or at least embrace Aria and give Jack a hearty handshake.

Free Will

Susan wiped her tears and sprang off the bed. "We have to make a list, John." She grabbed pen and paper from the desk in the corner of the bedroom, handed them to her husband, and began dictating. Before long the page was getting full and John was wondering how they would have time to gather everything on the list. "Don't worry," Susan told him. "This is going to happen, John." Before he knew it, she was on the phone, rallying the troops and handing out assignments.

Chapter Sixteen

Last Call

Tracy was waiting inside Liberty's when Jack and Aria entered and immediately directed them to the seating area opposite the bar, preferring not to have the bartender listen in on their conversation. Jack and Aria dutifully complied and plopped down on the large leather couch, where they were rewarded with glasses of wine from the bottle Tracy purchased minutes before.

"Not that it's not nice to see you . . . again. But what are you doing here?" Aria asked, while Tracy poured the wine.

Jack noted just a touch of stress in Aria's voice, as if Tracy's visit was not completely welcome. He decided to relieve some of the tension.

"Thanks for the wine, Tracy. It's really good."

Jack quickly emptied half his glass and was now coveting what was left in the bottle. He would have to control himself. *Sip. Sip.* The wine was delicious, and triggered a memory of the night before, when his quiet glass of wine was interrupted by an inter-collegiate row brought on by a disagreement over a girlfriend's level of promiscuity. Jack was confident that this time, so far as he could tell, his wine stood a good chance of *not* being flung from the table. He took a calm sip and reclined.

"You're welcome, Jack." To Jack's delight, Tracy refilled his glass before turning her attention back to her friend.

Free Will

"Well, if I'm being honest, I was just a little worried about . . . about you two, and I wanted to make sure you were still good." Tracy's worry was mostly, if not exclusively, for Aria, but she didn't want to be rude.

"You mean, like, you wanted to make sure we didn't jump off the bridge again?"

Jack got the sense that Aria was feeling a tad crowded by Tracy, that her friend had achieved an uncomfortable level of intrusiveness. He told himself to stay out of it. There was clearly a long and tangled history between them, and now was not the time to attempt an unraveling. He took another sip of wine, pleased that Tracy had rendered the glass bottomless.

"No, no, no. That's not it. Not at all. No." Tracy paused. "Well, maybe a little. But only a little. I mean, I didn't really think you guys would do it again."

"So, you drove back down here just to drink more wine and *not* to make sure we didn't jump off the bridge?" The pitch of Aria's voice escalated.

She was annoyed by Tracy's appearance, though not quite sure why, at least not exactly. For sure, she was exhausted and, as a result, it was possible for almost anything to annoy her. At the moment that thing happened to be her best friend. But she knew her ire resulted from more than just exhaustion. There was also the fact her friend was interrupting her "date" with Jack, a feeling which, coincidentally, was exacerbated by her exhaustion. A vicious circle.

Tracy relented. "Ok, fine. You got me. I was worried about my friend, meaning you, and her new boyfriend, meaning him." Tracy pointed at Jack with her thumb. "C'mon! Can you blame me? Look at what you've been through . . . what you've *both* been through."

Jack unintentionally joined the conversation by blurting out a response to Tracy's query. The words escaped before he could stop them.

"I think, if I'm being honest, I can see Tracy's point. You know . . . given the circumstances and all."

Jack was horrified by his intervention, more so because he was 100% sure he came in on the wrong side. But Aria, instead of getting angry, appeared to consider his point of view. He was sure of it when she set her wine on the table and proceeded to hug Tracy.

"You're a good friend, Tracy. Thank you for coming down here . . . again."

Vicious circle broken.

Tracy returned the hug. "Is there anything I can do for you . . . either of you?"

Jack was calm, sipping his wine, and feeling somewhat slighted at being left out of the love-fest underway at the other end of the couch. He shrugged it off, figuring correctly it was more important for Aria to put her friend's mind at ease than it was for him to receive his own set of hugs. The wine was enough, and Jack silently contemplated buying another bottle, though he wasn't sure they'd have time to drink it before he and Aria needed to leave.

It was in this moment of hugs and wine-induced self-reflection that River breached the threshold of the bar, entering from the sunlit sidewalk into the relative darkness of the interior. He gave his eyes a few seconds to adjust, but in the nearly empty void he easily recognized the three people sitting on the couch.

Girding his loins, River took a deep breath and took the few steps necessary to join Jack, Aria, and Tracy. He'd practiced his greeting on his way over from the coffee shop, but was now at a loss for words, and so found himself standing in front of the couch, staring at its occupants, mouth slightly agape.

Jack and Aria, of course, recognized River as the man they'd seen on and off since their morning trip to Coffee Emporium. Aria released

Tracy from their hug and turned toward the pudgy man in the brown suit and wrinkled trench coat.

"Can we help you?"

Aria had expected her question to be more expansive, more comprehensive, something along the lines of, "Who are you and why are you here?" or, for a dramatic flair, "What is the meaning of this?" After all, as she understood it, this guy had been following them around for hours. But the wine was working its magic, and she didn't feel agitated with the intruder so much as curious. And though she didn't feel her question to be satisfyingly penetrating, it turned out to be the right one, because it opened the floodgates of River's brain, and he began to spew.

"Um, I'm River Van Beek and I work for the Enquirer. I've been trying to talk to you two all day, well, mostly trying to find you, and *then* talk to you. I thought I knew who you were at one point and then I wasn't so sure. See, I was reading the Sheriff's desk blotter and there was this story about how there might be an alligator, or maybe a lungfish, crawling out of the Ohio River and then it turned out to be just two human beings and there was some information on the human beings that crawled out of the river and, you know, that sort of thing is really interesting because it doesn't happen very often, I mean, people falling into the river and all, so I started following up on the story and, you know, when I started asking around it led me to you guys and I've been trying all day to . . . I don't even know. At first I thought what I should do is just talk to you but you didn't answer your door so then I figured I'd try to follow you around to see if you, you know, maybe tried to jump in the river again but you both walk so fast and I had trouble keeping up and then I almost got hit by a car and . . . well, you know, I'm not even sure what I'm doing at this point but I was across the street in the coffee shop and I saw you guys walk into the bar and I figured, you know, what the heck? Maybe I can get them to talk to me, even though they don't have to. I'm not the cops or anything, just a reporter. I can't make anybody tell me anything but I was hoping you would . . . talk to me, I mean."

A pregnant silence marked the end of River's oration as everyone, including River, digested the stream of word vomit. Jack was the first to finish processing.

"So . . . it's River, right? So, River, are you saying you just want to talk to us about last night?"

River, apparently having used up all the words he had available, nodded in the affirmative.

"Ok, then, do you have any specific questions you'd like to ask? Is there anything you'd like to know that you didn't see on the Sheriff's blotter?" Jack had no idea what information a Sheriff's blotter contained, his experience with the phrase being limited to what he'd learned from *Law and Order* reruns on late-night television.

It took River a moment to formulate a response to Jack's question. He hadn't expected Jack to be so straightforward and found himself reconsidering his initial "beat around the bush until you get some answers" stratagem in favor of a more direct question/answer tactic. It made his brain hurt, just a little, but a question finally emerged, and it happened to be *the* question.

River took a deep breath. "Did you guys jump off the bridge on purpose last night?"

Jack, Aria, and Tracy startled, none expecting the man in the ill-fitting suit to dive right in. In an unexpected fit of protective pique, Tracy found herself not only feeling defensive toward her friend, but Jack as well. How dare this man, this dumpy ragamuffin, interfere with their lives?

"Excuse me . . . um, River," she emphasized his name condescendingly. "Who are you to ask them this question?'

River, characteristically self-conscious, did his best to stick to the facts. "Well, ma'am, like I said, I'm a reporter for the Enquirer, and this seems like a story. And, like I said, you know, they don't have to answer." River paused. "For all I know, they could have done it on a dare."

Silence again ensued. Tracy, now full of righteous indignation, did not expect such a straight answer to her straight question and, as a result, had no proper retort. She let River's words hang in the air somewhere over the coffee table while they, as a collective, quietly wondered where they could go from there. Aria stepped into the wordless void.

"River, would you like a glass of wine?"

River looked at his watch, even though he wasn't sure *why* he found it necessary to do so. And, upon discovering his watch provided him no help whatsoever, answered simply.

"Yes. I mean, yes, please."

Tracy, still indignant but now breathing normally, motioned to the bartender for another bottle. She didn't really believe River deserved any of it, but her friend had extended the offer and she wasn't going to be uncivilized.

"May I sit?" River trod more miles that day than he had in years, probably since high school, and his legs were feeling the effects. Without waiting for permission, he sank into a comfy leather chair. He sipped the wine and waited, hoping he wouldn't have to ask *the* question again.

Aria and Jack nodded at one another. Reflected in the nod was the agreement they would again tell the lie they'd crafted after escaping the river, the lie they'd so far told everyone, except Tracy, who asked. Jack began the well-practiced recitation, describing for River how he and Aria were on a date, about how they'd had a very nice evening and getting to know one another beyond their established bartender/customer relationship, and how they thought walking across the iconic suspension bridge in the snow would be romantic.

Aria took over, describing the quiet attraction she and Jack had shared for the past year, how they'd leaned across the bar to kiss each other one busy Friday night, and about how nothing had happened since, at least not until last night.

For the next part, the slipping-off-an-icy-bridge part, Jack and Aria tag-teamed River with their own versions of how it felt to fall toward the water and how they escaped from it, only to be harassed and plucked from the riverbank by sheriffs, paramedics, and firemen. In a rapid-fire staccato, the storytelling now bounced back and forth between Aria and Jack as they recounted the tasing, the ride in the ambulance, the drunken priest, and how Jack spotted the riotous college students in the hospital waiting room.

The suicide test was purposely omitted.

As was the pharmacy adventure.

And how they hid, and had sex, in a storage closet.

And how they drank in the chapel with the priest.

River's note-taking was barely able to keep up and, at the end, he was enthralled and overjoyed—enthralled by the love story Jack and Aria were telling, and overjoyed that he would be allowed to tell the same story, and though he wasn't quite sure which section of the newspaper it would fit, he was almost sure the Enquirer had never published anything like it. He looked up from his notebook as he finished taking his last note.

"Well, thank you both very much for sharing that story with me. I hope you don't mind if I share it with my readers. This is the kind of thing that people would really be interested in."

Aria was surprised. "Really? Why?"

Free Will

River didn't hesitate. "Well, it's a love story, isn't it? Look what you've been through together, and now you're sitting here, in the bar where it all started, still holding hands. I'll be honest with you, at first I suspected you all were attempting a double suicide, but, you know, clearly you weren't. It was an accident."

River, to his credit, made a point *not* to mention he'd studied up on the accident that killed Jack's nephew, Troy.

Jack felt strangely defensive. "Well, River, what makes you so sure it *wasn't* a suicide attempt?"

Aria squeezed Jack's hand. Tracy looked alarmed.

Jack continued. "Not that it was, of course. I guess I'm just wondering why it's so clear?"

"Oh, well, I suppose because anybody who was really trying to kill themselves by jumping off that bridge would probably have gone all the way to the top."

Jack was startled, but continued his questioning despite Aria's tightening grip. "What do you mean, 'all the way to the top'?"

"Well, I mean all the way to the top of one of the towers."

Jack was now dumbfounded. "Top of the towers?"

"Well, yeah. I did a little research; from where you jumped the bridge is normally about 65 feet above the water. If you had climbed the staircase to the top of the tower, you would have gotten at least another hundred feet, maybe more. I mean, it wouldn't be easy to get to the stairs, they've seen to that, but if somebody really wanted a good chance at killing themselves, that would do it. Don't you think?"

As an engineer, Jack knew exactly what River was talking about, and was getting angry about it. Why didn't *he* think of that when he was making his plans the week before? How was it that this bumbling, pudgy reporter understood more about the mechanics of throwing oneself off a bridge than Jack? He was now angry at himself, questioning his own competence and poor planning. Had he not been serious about his desired outcome? Had he purposely ignored the obvious in favor of giving himself a chance to survive? He couldn't be sure, and he wasn't about to vocalize his own doubts, at least not with anyone other than Aria, and maybe not even her.

But, he thought to himself, if not Aria, who? There really was no one else, no one who understood everything the way she did. If he were to bounce the idea of his misplaced disappointment off anyone, it was Aria. And it was at that moment the grinding of her nails into the palm of his hand finally registered. He pulled himself together. He needed to gracefully, unsuspiciously, back out of the conversation.

"Ah, of course. You must learn a lot on your job, River." Jack's teeth, ever so slightly, clenched. "Obviously, only an idiot wouldn't have thought about increasing their chances of success by utilizing that extra height."

River smiled, oblivious to Jack's disappointment at having abandoned everything he'd ever learned about physics.

Aria could take no more. "Ok, well, it was very nice to meet you, River, but we have to go. We've got plans with family tonight. Do you have everything you need?"

"Oh, yeah, I'm good. But I just thought of something. If you haven't already, you both might want to let your families know what happened to you last night. I think the last thing you'd want is for them to read about it in the news first. After all, you guys will be celebrities after this. This story will go viral!"

Aria held some doubt as to the level of interest their story might garner on social media, but regardless took River's point and responded while Jack brooded over his failure to properly execute his own suicide.

"Wow, hadn't really thought about that."

Free Will

Aria stood, dragging Jack off the couch as well. Tracy and River followed suit.

River was the first to leave, awkwardly turning away from the people he'd been observing on and off all day and from whom he was given the good news that his persistence had not been in vain, that he had a story after all. That story, published the following Tuesday in the Local section of the Enquirer, would earn River a promotion and be the biggest story he would ever write, getting picked up by the national news services and, yes, going viral. Sort of. River, on the advice of his editor, Perry, substituted pseudonyms for Jack and Aria, thereby offering them a layer of protection from intrusions by meddlesome, stalking types.

Tracy waited for the door to close behind River before offering her own goodbyes, which came in the form of hugs and a promise to see them later at Aria's parents' house. She started her engine as Aria and Jack turned the corner, heading back to his place where they would get ready for the rest of their evening.

They were happy to be back at Jack's, the interior comfortably unlit and lacking expectations of any kind beyond getting ready to meet each other's families. Jack offered the first shower to Aria, who suggested they conserve resources and shower together. Jack reluctantly begged off on the joint shower. He had something to do.

3:45 PM
I know you won't read this until later (I'll make sure of that!)
We'll be leaving in just a few minutes, so I don't have much time for this.
But I wanted to write to you before we leave.
I wanted to write to you one more time before everything changes for us.
That will start happening as soon as we walk out the door.

It will especially change for me, I think.
But we're both in it, aren't we? We're in this together.
I don't know what will happen tonight, or tomorrow, or the day after.
But I know that I'm not alone, not anymore.
And, with any luck, never again.
I'm kicking myself for wasting all this time, for not kissing you again when I had the chance, for not getting out of my own way, for not taking the time to find you before you found me.
Oh, and if I didn't say it yet, thank you for that, for finding me, I mean.
For saving me by almost killing yourself.
I couldn't ask anymore of a first date than that. We'll see how the second one goes.
I'm counting tonight as that second date, by the way.
Ok – I think you just turned the shower off.
My turn.

Aria stood in the foyer, by the open door, looking back at Jack. He seemed paralyzed, unable to move. They were both now clean, both now presentable. Aria suspected she knew what was going on in Jack's head and so let him stand there, knowing he would move when he was able to do so. Still, time was passing. She took the knob in one hand, opened the door, and extended her free hand to Jack.

"Take my hand, Jack. I'll drive."

John Current stood in the kitchen, examining the provisions that had already started arriving, the provisions that would greet the evening's guests when they arrived. If they arrived. Of that he was still not

Free Will

sure. He wouldn't blame his son for not showing up though he would allow himself to be devastated if that were the case. He had done what he could do, at least for now, so he stared at the food, the wine, the napkins he'd laid out.

A moment came when he felt a hand in his own, a hand of unmistakable provenance; a hand he'd spent decades fitting into his own. His wife pulled him to her, pulled him down to kiss his cheek.

"He'll be here."

About the Author

Mark E. Scott lives in the Over The Rhine neighborhood of downtown Cincinnati.

Upcoming New Release!

MARK E. SCOTT'S

KING OF PERU

Matt Obrodnick started hearing a voice, one he couldn't recognize or escape, and sounded vaguely Spanish…

Follow the ex-marine as he navigates college classes, a chain-smoking roommate, love interests, and a ruthless, long-dead conquistador who wants Matt to pick up where he left off.

For more information visit: www.SpeakingVolumes.us

Now Available!

MARK E. SCOTT'S

A DAY IN THE LIFE
BOOK ONE – BOOK TWO – BOOK THREE

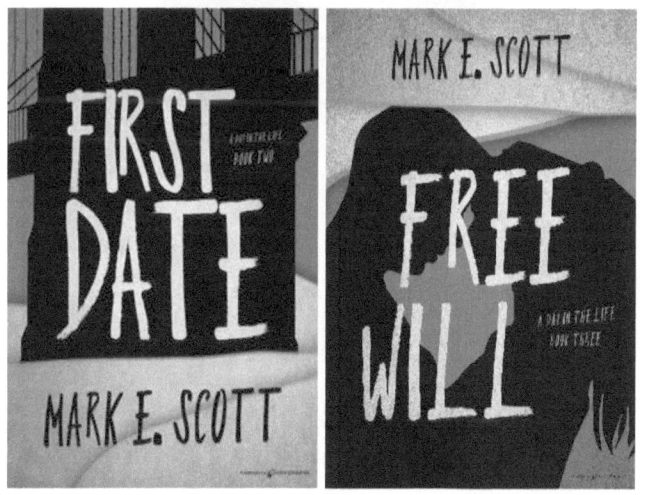

**For more information
visit:** www.SpeakingVolumes.us

Now Available!

TONI GLICKMAN'S

BITCHES OF FIFTH AVENUE
BOOK ONE – BOOK TWO – BOOK THREE

For more information visit: www.SpeakingVolumes.us

Now Available!

JORDAN S. KELLER'S

ASHES OVER AVALON
BOOK ONE – BOOK TWO – BOOK THREE

**For more information
visit:** www.SpeakingVolumes.us

Now Available!

AWARD-WINNING AUTHOR
CHARLENE WEXLER

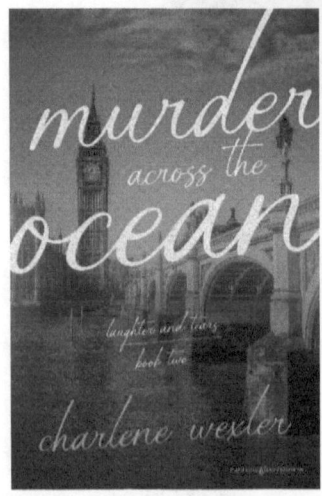
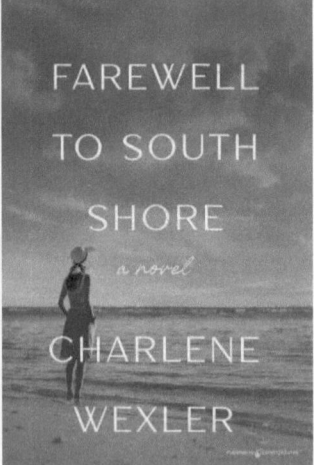

For more information visit: www.SpeakingVolumes.us

www.ingramcontent.com/pod-product-compliance
Lightning Source LLC
LaVergne TN
LVHW041703060526
838201LV00043B/557